HOMEWARD BOUND AND OTHER STORIES

EGILL ATLASON

Contents

Homeward Bound

I must have watched the show during every waking moment that semester, except when I was lecturing. It wasn't highbrow. In fact, it was downright chthonic in how it appealed to our baser sensibilities. Now, I have always had a predisposition for that kind of literature, but this was something else. So, while other lecturers regurgitated Dante and Shakespeare, I discussed Coleridge and psychopomps. Thinking back on it, I suppose this kind of show was bound to come up in one of my classes.

I was in the middle of explaining the significance of the Albatross when a certain Shaun yelled over the class, "Mr. Newman, you're always telling us about this weird literature stuff that no one reads. Why don't you ever talk about something nice, like My Little Pony? That's weird enough, and it was written this century."

I figured I'd tease him a little. "Everyone! On account of Shaun, you are all to watch My Little Pony for the next class."

They laughed because they knew I never meant for them to watch it. Certainly, I never meant to. It was simply a matter of curiosity.

The Show was beyond art. It perfectly enounced all those things we pathetically delegate to the terms loneliness, the human condition, or love. Soon I knew everything about the tribulations of Twilight Sparkle and the Mane six. I stopped going to insignificant lectures, and rather than attending my weekly lunch with Professor Gustav, I stayed at home and watched My Little Pony.

And I would have been content to hole myself up in my apartment, except for the knowledge that none of my essays on the subject would have been published. Who would publish an essay on the auteur's influence on MLP, or Fluttershy's obvious role as a Christ-figure? No, any serious exploration of the show would have ruined my reputation.

Then around the Canterlot wedding, must have been April 2012, I noticed news coverage of Bronies; that's what they called the fans. They were strange creatures. Fox news was worried they were sexualizing the horses. It gave me an idea. I rushed from the couch to a stack of papers I had on my desk, knocking over an empty pizza box. Sifting, flinging paper to the far ends of my apartment, I found a brochure I'd come across a few months back: Bronycon. In this post-modern age, academics were only interested in audiences. That would give me enough distance from the subject matter for an essay to be respectable.

On the day of the conference, I took the subway to 42nd street, where I hailed a cab. A couple next to me was consulting a map, arguing about whether they had time to visit Madame Tussauds. She held an M&M figurine, but she might as well have held a sign saying, "We're tourists!"

"Where to?" the driver said.

"Meadowlands Exposition Centre."

The radio was playing a duet. They sang about being a rock. About building walls. It was despicable pop culture as far as I was concerned.

"Could you turn that off?" I said.

He adjusted his rear view mirror to look at me. "You don't like Tom and Jerry?"

I furrowed my brow until he turned it off.

We didn't speak until we came to the place. Then he looked me over, my herring-bone and satchel. "Are you sure this is your stop?"

I handed him the exact fare.

Hanging above the entrance was a banner with big colorful letters, BronyCon. And the pilgrims it amassed were no less colorful. They all had some indicator, some picture on their t-shirt, or a hat fashioned as the face of one of the ponies. Seen from here, it was almost beautiful in a way, all the colors. But I remembered Hylas and was careful to gaze from afar.

A man of my age had on a blue wig, out of which he had taken some hairs to make a makeshift moustache; he wore a suit and had on a monocle: Fancy Pants. Yet another was cosplaying Discord. Disparate monstrous body parts were glued to the man. Horns and claws, a tail, and a fake beard. There was a walking effigy of Pinkie Pie, although rather too furry to claim realism; her head was that of a football mascot to boot. She was offering free hugs by means of a sign.

On my right was a group of people singing the smile song. If you have ever heard the smile song, you know the point is not to heed the obvious shamelessness of it. But these dejected creatures were too ill-fitted for good company to manage that. Awkward would be too kind of a term for them.

Shuffling through the crowd, I entered the convention. Once inside, I was assailed on all sides by sales booths and body odor. They sold countless identity markers: t-shirts, pins, hats, professional and home-made pastiches, everything from sketches to posters to statues.

I got my notebook up and tapped on it with my pen, but I could hardly look at the crowd. I doubted if any of them tried to fight the maelstrom that is the show to maintain grace. So, I walked past the statues instead. They had a whole line of tables just for stat-ues, and if you wanted to get a good look, you had to squeeze between two social neophytes. In the middle of a sea of statues was a true work of art: a handmade figurine of Princess Celestia. The detail was exquisite. Her blue and pink mane looped around her as if suspended at that short moment in a ribbon dance where the ribbon takes its form and should drop, but this one never did. It would serve as exhibit A of the Bronies' dedication.

I coughed a little to get the cashier's attention. She was a young girl, a little homely but cheerful. "Excuse me, I would like to buy that statue."

I expected her to judge my looks as the taxi driver had done, but if she did, she hid it perfectly behind her smile. "Sure thing, mister. Would you like that wrapped up?"

"Yes, please." Anything to hide it.

"This is our most expensive figurine, did you come from far away to buy this?"

"No, I live in the city."

"Oh yeah, what borough?" She looked me in the eyes, holding one finger on a fold in the wrapping paper.

"The Bronx." I glanced at the statue.

She focused on her work. "Hey, you're just one step from being a Brony, then."

"Excuse me?"

"You know, because if you take the x and change it to a y then Bronx is Brony." She handed me a box all wrapped up with pink ribbons, almost as embarrassing as the statue inside. "It's just a silly joke."

I yanked the box from her. "You shouldn't be interrogating people like that."

She stopped smiling. "I'm sorry, sir, I was just making small talk."

As soon as I had paid her, I walked to the other side of the convention until a conga line of costumed attendants blocked my path. On the other side of a large black partition, I heard: "Let the chaos begin."

I shuffled into a makeshift auditorium crammed with people. Through some nudging, I found myself a bit of space in the corner. On stage was the man who voiced Discord, the mischievous amalgam of beasts: de Lancie.

He stroked his chin. "A few months ago, I got asked to voice a kids' show, and not three months later, I have four hundred emails in my inbox. Now, I was of the understanding that it was a show for little girls, but these were not little girls messaging me."

The whole crowd laughed in a self-aware fashion.

"Since then, I've slowly been getting a sense of what this community is. And you aren't the sort of people who they say you are on the news. In fact, one of the news stations that had the audacity to cover you the other day, I daresay should not call themselves a news station. So now, during this convention, you get a chance to define who you are rather than those jerks. And I'm telling you, we need so much more of you. This world needs more of you."

They applauded this. An empty acclamation was what these lost souls wanted. As if a grown man can dress up as a pony and expect to be cured of his conscience with a hug, that it's the judgment of others afflicting him, that he isn't desecrating his object of admiration by attempting to... merge with it. These people were an open book, and I decided not to interview them. I could gain no insight from a cog. They would tell me about their dejected life, their relief in finding the show, hesitation and sense of belonging in the machine. I might learn something from a mechanic, such as de Lancie.

De Lancie went straight from the panel

to write autographs, and I had to stand in line for a full fifteen minutes before I could talk to him.

I had my notebook out to sketch our conversation. "Good afternoon, Mr. Lancie."

"Hey there." He grabbed my notebook and signed his name on the first page.

"I was hoping I could ask you a few questions."

"There will be a panel for that later."

He had hardly handed me back my notebook before the next person pushed me out of the way. "I was thinking something more like an interview," I said.

"Mhm," he said.

"I'll meet you in your green room," I blurted out as someone nearly elbowed me in the face trying to get past me.

"Yeah, exactly," he said while writing the next autograph.

I must have spent half an hour looking for the green room. It was a little room on the second floor. The names de Lancie and Tara Strong were posted on the door. Inside there was a standing mirror, a partition, a couch and a coffee table. On the table was a vegetable platter and a stack of paper. I sat down on the couch and got out my statue. Before I had gotten far unwrapping the thing, I noticed what it said on those papers on the coffee table: MLP season 3 episode 2: The Crystal Empire, Part 2: Tara Strong. I put down my statue, opened the script in the middle and read from the top.

Princess Celestia: What are you doing here?

Twilight: I don't know. I opened the door and…

Princess Celestia: And now you must go.

Twilight: Go Where?

Princess Celestia: I doesn't matter to me. You failed the test, Twilight.

Twilight: I don't understand. The test?

Princess Celestia: Not only will you not move on to the next level of your studies, you won't continue your studies at all.

Twilight: You didn't say anything about no longer being your student if I failed.

Princess Celestia: Didn't I?

Twilight: But what do I do now?

I was positively shaking. What bliss, what privilege to read a script from the next season while everyone else would have to wait until fall. I almost didn't hear two voices approaching, two voices I recognized well.

Ashamed of my transgression, I returned the script and hid behind the partition in a matter of seconds.

"Why do you think those guys like the show so much?" De Lancie said.

"Because it's incredibly well written. And fantastically voiced, might I add?" Tara Strong said. Her voice had a buoyancy to it.

"I suppose." He paused. "Don't you think they're a bit weird, though?"

"Yeah, and a bit deviant too." She put all the emphasis on "deviant."

"Exactly."

Tara didn't miss a beat. "I happen to like that about them."

De Lancie chuckled a little. In the following minute, the only sounds from the other side of the partition were a few taps on the table and then the crinkling of wrapping paper.

"Is this your statue?" de Lancie said.

"No."

"Wow, look at that price tag."

It wasn't that much. Not for research material.

"Oh, my goodness," Tara said.

I heard him put it back on the table. "I'm just happy they have each other. I mean, you can't justify this statute if you don't have the community. Who's even gonna make it? Without the community, you're a grown man watching a children's show, but with them, you're a Brony. That has to account for something."

We all sat in silence for a great deal of time before de Lancie said, "We should get going, shouldn't we?"

They slammed the door behind them. The sound echoed in my mind for a while as I stood frozen behind the partition. In a sense I had had my interview. It wouldn't translate well into academia, though. "Strength in numbers: The Brony community justifies abnormal behavior." No, it wasn't that. It wasn't group mentality. It wasn't regression, or the great mother, or transgression, or patriarchy; none of the academic idiosyncrasies.

I left the room without my statue. The crowd in the main hall was a bundle of disheveled, lost people, banding around a chthonic ooze, a whirlpool sucking you in because once in it, you couldn't exit easily. But is it not like that with everything we profess to love? Should this be any better or worse? I saw that ridiculous Pinkie Pie at the end of the hall and walked toward it. Are we not obligated to lay down at the feet of whatever fancy our impressionable minds and our hapless circumstances put before us? I stood before the furry effigy, laid out my arms in hopeless surrender, and hugged it.

Diana

She was bald. Not like cancer bald. More like… Britney bald. Also, she wore this gorgeous pink slip-dress so you could see all her tattoos.

"This is Dolores," Carrie said. Her parents were away for the weekend, and we were celebrating that.

I put out my hand to greet her. "Diana."

"Do you wanna touch it?" Dolores gestured to her head.

"No, that's fine." I put my hand down.

"Your loss." She looked around the room as if she was just now taking it in. It was a suburban house painted all white. And most of the people looked like you put a bunch of modern art in a blender and taught it how to dance. The number of ear gauges – a horrible term – must have been well over the statistical average.

Dolores looked back at us. "I'm going dancing, girlfriends." As she walked away, she did something with her hands I could only assume to be an obscene gesture.

I turned to Carrie. "Where'd you even meet this girl?"

"Be nice. And try to mingle. You never mingle." She gestured with her empty glass and left me.

Whatever. I wasn't really into this artsy crowd. Didn't feel like being lectured on the benefits of reiki. I guess it might have been fun to speculate about what they were overcompensating for with their orange overalls and layers upon layers of sarcasm, but that was about it. The guy Dolores was dancing with was kind of cute, though. How could they dance to that music? It didn't even sound like music; it sounded like the Seinfeld theme was having a stroke. I looked at her crazy bald head and stroked my amber locks. Somehow I always figured you were supposed to keep your hair long and sleek. I finished my beer and went to the fridge where the only beer that wasn't an IPA was some off-brand Lager. So, I grabbed that and sat back down on the couch.

Dolores plopped down on the couch next to me. "Back so soon?" I asked.

She looked through me. "You're funny."

She had a few tattoos on her arms. Three birds taking flight, some quote, and a few white lines running parallel to her wrist. I grabbed her left arm and pointed to the birds. "What does this one mean?"

"It's because I want to be like a bird, so I can fly away."

I was caressing her arm, even though I wasn't that drunk. "I don't think I could ever get a tattoo. I get so sick of things the best I could do would be a painting. That way, if I every started hating it, I could just throw it away."

"I guess."

I read the quote out loud. "Everything has beauty, but not everyone can see. Who said that?"

"Confucius."

"You read a lot of Confucius?"

She yawned. "Not really. Just liked that quote."

She leaned closer to me, and I started stroking her head. I don't know why, just felt like it. And it wasn't awkward or anything. I felt I knew Dolores better than anyone. As if her naked head was some crazy symbol or something. Like I told you, I'm not into that artsy stuff, and a bald head is just a bald head, but I don't know; it felt different in the moment.

Dolores flashed me this cheeky smile. "You're alright." She reached up and kissed me on the cheek before she ran back to the dance floor.

I must have watched her dance for half an hour because when I slinked out, it was almost two am. Walking home, I had this urge to make a snow angel. To make some temporary mark. I lay down on the ground and moved my hands and feet up and down. Lying there, I thought I had no tattoos because I was a coward. That I could never wear my heart on my sleeve like that.

Jacob's Windmill

"**O**kay, hear me out. What if you could go back into your old body but with your current knowledge and social skills? Huh, Jacob?" Joe poked me in the arm and gulped down his beer.

We were sitting in the back of the bar. Logan's place was a local place with eternally dimmed lights, one kind of whisky (Jack Daniels) and a regular in every seat at the bar. While the jukebox blared "American Pie," Joe was on his second rant, and Trish was staring down her makeshift sangria – they had no fruit.

Joe said, "You'd be a total boy genius; just strut in there with an adult mind like, hey, I'm here to ace all the tests. And you'd get all the girls because no one else would have any class."

"I guess you could really steer things in the right direction," I said.

He stood up. Joe was a real tower, so you noticed when he stood up. On sunny days his shiny bald head could blind you if you caught it at the wrong angle. "Exactly. You'd get this crazy head start. Like how we didn't know that this place doesn't card until we were eighteen. We could have been here at least a year sooner. Could have had the whole crew in here."

He was talking about everyone who moved away for university. "How would that be helpful?"

"He's got you there," Trish said and gave me the eye.

Joe said, "Well, you could also, like, work out and stuff."

The jukebox switched over to "Summer of '69," and Joe roared, "Yes."

I answered with an equally resounding, "No."

"Come on, the man is a national treasure!"

They sang that atrocious song. I gestured to my cigarettes and walked outside. Lighting up, I figured I might as well head home. Besides, that way, I wouldn't have to walk Trish home. She was great and all, but she had that little kid at home. Poor thing. There was a full moon out, and it was about as hot as it gets up here.

We lived pretty far up north; you wouldn't know the place. One of those abandoned mining towns in rural Canada. It's pretty and all, but you could drive for a solid day in any direction and get nowhere. The thing is, I could never get used to even the few degrees we got in the summer. I wanted it to snow. I always liked walking alone in the snow. So, what I did, I sort of imagined I was catching snowflakes on my tongue. I must have looked half crazy, sticking my tongue out at the town as I stumbled home.

* * *

I woke up to the tumultuous roar of my mother vacuuming, with a headache and sweaty sheets. "Mom, do you have to vacuum right now?"

"If I wasn't the only one who cleaned this place, then maybe I could vacuum at your leisure," she yelled from the hallway.

I glanced at my alarm clock. "Mom, it is 8 AM on a fucking Sunday."

She practically hissed. "Don't swear at me!"

"I'm a grown man, I'll talk, however –"

She poked her head through my door. She wasn't too old, but she already had some grey hair. "You're not a grown anything, and while you're living under my roof, you'll do as I say." She slammed the door.

I didn't know what the hell happened, but at least she stopped vacuuming. Before I knew it, old Sandman had knocked me out again.

When I woke up again, I stole into the kitchen for a cup of coffee. I liked a cup of black coffee in the morning to get properly jolted. It became a habit after I worked at the garage and had to keep up with the older guys. I snuck back into my room, flumped into my computer chair and played Counter Strike for maybe a couple of hours.

"Dinner!"

Sweet. I finished the round and ran to the kitchen table. On the table was a pot full of beef stew and three bowls. Weird. I thought she stopped doing that a few months after the old man had gone. I scooped some stew on to my plate – it was thick enough I couldn't make out any of the ingredients – and started walking back to my room.

"Don't you want to eat at the table?" she said.

"No." My voice cracked.

She put on this nutty passive-aggressive stance where she leaned her head back so far I thought she would fall off her chair. And then she always complained about having a sore neck.

I hadn't eaten at the table in forever. "You know I like eating by myself."

"Since when?" she said.

"Since forever." I took a decisive step back.

"Jacob Matthew Barrie, we are going to sit down and eat as a family."

"Whatever." I walked away.

As I was turning around, she grabbed my arm and pretty violently at that. "You either sit down right now, or you aren't eating."

I didn't know what had gotten into her, but there is a way to respond to that kind of shit. "Screw your crummy stew then!"

I put my plate down, all calm and collected, put on my coat and walked out the door. There's really just one main road out here and three places to get food. The minimart, Wendy's, and chicken wings at Logan's place; wasn't too early for a drink.

It stays bright pretty much all evening up here in the springtime, so you could really see all the cracks in the place. The neon flickered, and the one ashtray outside was always full. A dive like that should never be in full view.

Logan himself was outside having a smoke. He had these crazy shoulders, and he stood like he was trying to keep the damn things as far away from each other as possible. Kept his hair neat and medium length, thick sideburns, and his mouth was always a little open.

"Hey Logan, is anyone in yet?"

He took a long drag of his cigarette. "You're Mason's kid, right?"

"Fuck no." I didn't like to associate with the old man.

"He was causing a ruckus here last night."

"Quit playing around, Logan." There was no way the old man was back in town, and I didn't appreciate whatever Logan was getting at. I walked toward the door.

Out of nowhere, he put his hand on my chest. "Can't come in here, kid."

"What did you just call me, you boomer fuck?"

He smiled all the way to his stupid sideburns. "What did you just call me?"

I pushed his hand away. "Fuck this bit, I'm going inside."

I hadn't taken a step when he straight-up pushed me to the ground. That cuntshit went too far. I was gonna call Joe, and we'd make him pay. Burn the place down for all I cared. I'd FaceTime him right there in front of Logan even. I stood up and got my phone out of my pocket. I had a block of a Nokia phone in my hand. Why did I have a Nokia in my hand?

"Just you and your fucking sideburns wait right there." I backed away from Logan toward home.

Just had to get my actual phone to call Joe, except I thought I'd thrown away the

Nokia. Opened the front door and stroked my head as I walked into the house. Did I shave my head last night? Just had to splash my face with some water. I kind of fell on the bathroom door. But I got to the sink and saw myself in the mirror. I had this baby face with zits and the buzz cut I had in high school. Had to sit down, so I sat on the edge of the bathtub and let myself sink down.

I sat there pinching myself in the arm for a while. Was I really a teenager? Was this a ridiculously vivid lucid dream or a once-in-a-lifetime poetic shot at changing the past like in those awful pre-teen movies? Either way, I blew it playing video games all day.

"I'll call Veronica," I said out loud, like a crazy person. If Veronica was around, then I was really in the past.

Her number was in my phone. You know, I hardly ever called anyone anymore. What a shame. Texting is so impersonal.

"Hello."

I sat up in the tub. "Hey, Veronica? It's Jacob."

"Hi…"

"Fucktits, it's really good to hear your voice. Can you come see me?"

She was tittering nervously on the other

end. It was actually nice to hear. "I'm at a stupid dinner thing with my parents," she said.

"Well, then after that?"

"That's too late. You'll see me at school tomorrow."

"Look, I don't know if I'm going to be at school tomorrow. I'll come over in an hour."

I had almost put the phone back in my pocket when I heard her yell, "No, I can't have a boy over at night."

Maybe I was coming on a little strong. "You're right. I'll talk to you later. You have a good night in the meantime, alright."

"Goodbye." She hung up.

God, I couldn't believe it. Veronica. We used to hang out a little, but I never made a move on her. Like she just got away from me. She'd hung out with some rough people a few years ago. Which would be a couple of years from now? Anyway, she ran away from home, threw away her phone, and nobody had heard from her since. I didn't care if this was all a dream if I could meet Veronica.

The stew was already down the drain, so I made myself a bologna sandwich. My room was just about how I left it in the present. I guess the pile of dirty laundry was a little smaller, and I could still make out all the things I had swept under the bed. For the past few years, I have been caring for a few consecutive laurel plants. This one was already withering.

I may have slept that night. I felt crazy restless even before going to bed. I played some more Counter Strike. In bed, I conjured up all these crazy fantasies about owning the school tomorrow. Anyone try to square up to me, I'd outsmart the hell out of them. I'd even square up to the teachers. Before I knew it, the alarm rang. The digital clock had the date below the time, and I grabbed that sucker with both hands: still the past. I showered away a double case of night sweats and chucked my schoolbag on my back. The damn thing almost broke me in half; I had a library in there. Once I'd emptied the bag of everything but one notebook and a pencil case, I rushed out.

The school was a brick monstrosity. It had this unique smell. I don't know if it was that combination of prepubescent sweat, old bricks, and acquiescence, but it didn't smell like anywhere else. I sort of roamed around the place until I found my class.

They were all huddled up in these nonsensical groups. Artsy kids, pretty girls, the bikers, my boys Joe and Eric. I wondered if and why that happened in every high school. It's almost like the teenage paranoia that people are always judging you and personal change is impossible is a self-fulfilling prophesy. You simplify yourself into a pre-made identity to create a superficial connection with a few other people. What you're really doing is creating a shell around yourself to let people attack instead of the real you.

I walked up to the girls. "Ladies."

They all looked up at the same time. I guess I wasn't talking to them much at the time. Meanwhile, Joe was beckoning me over with all the passion of a madman.

I put up my index finger to the girls. "Excuse me."

My boys were just on the opposite side of the hall. I'd have so much time to hang out with them. "What's up?"

"What are you doing?" Joe said. It was weird seeing him. He had these noodle arms and wore a baggy t-shirt. Kind of twitchy, not his arrogant self at all.

"Well, I was thinking I might talk to the girls."

"You were just gonna walk up to them and talk to them?"

"Yeah."

Joe was having half a panic attack. He used to be so awkward before he got buffed. I figured I had better change the subject. "What are we doing after school?"

"We're going to the drop house," Eric said. He always wore this green puff ball hat, making his hair stand out from under it like Jim from the Office. And he had this whine to his voice like he wanted to pick a fight, but you knew he'd just run away. I stopped hanging out with him around the end of high school.

I had forgotten about the drop house. It was this windmill that some old looney built practically next to our school just after the mine closed. Of course, we were way too far north, so all his crops died, and the windmill stood like a testament to this guy's crazy optimism. The guy was dead and all, so the place was locked, to begin with, but after we broke the lock a few times, his son gave up trying to keep us out. Still, you had to hide everything you kept there because otherwise, the looney's spawn would take it. Or at least that was the excuse when someone took Kevin's Penthouse. The name was because of all these holes and hills the old looney had made. It's anyone's guess why he did it, although we think he meant to make dirt walls to shield his crops. Anyway, we used to take our bikes and jump from the high points to the low points. In some places, you'd drop down like five feet and just hope you had your nuts far away from your saddle. The place was demolished, and the terrain was flattened around the time we finished high school. That would be in a couple of years, probably.

"That's perfect." I turned back to the girls. "Hi again. The guys and I were wondering if you would join us at the drop house after school."

Joanne answered for them. "You want us to go to that dirty mill where you go to gay out?" Joanne ended up a boring desk clerk trying to eat herself to death. Fat lot of good a university education will do you.

"Suck my clit, Joanne." You should have seen her face. It was like her father told her he never loved her or something. "Just come hang out with us once, and if you hate it, you never have to do it again."

I guess she wasn't used to agreeing because she took forever to answer. "Fine."

"Great."

The bell rang, and we all sat down in our respective seats; it was Pavlovian as hell. The teacher, Diane – we were supposed to call her by her last name, but we never did – always had to spend the first three minutes of the day quieting the class. She handed us a paper: 10th-grade history, midterm. This would be easy; I'd already aced history.

I finished the test in twenty minutes flat and looked around the classroom for the remaining twenty. Maybe I'd pursue my studies and become the next Einstein; I had this great head start on everyone. Veronica had this really cute way of chewing on her pencil. She would never chew it in the same place for more than a couple of nibbles. So, she was constantly looking for new places to chew on, feeling around the pencil with her mouth. She had this figure too. Perfect bubbly butt. Waist made for grabbing. When she figured out she was beautiful, she became a different person, but for now, she was doing all these exquisite stretches, unaware of the commotion she was stirring in me.

"All right, kids, put down your pencils," Diane said.

After an equally dreamy math class, we went to recess, where us guys sat outside on the steps where they took the school picture. We formed a semicircle like a regular council.

"What was that Caravaggio on the test?" Joe said.

"David and Goliath?" Eric said.

"Yeah, David with the head of Goliath," Larry said, and about half the guys nodded.

I said Young Bacchus. It was the only Caravaggio I remembered, but she'd probably give me credit for that.

"What happened to Lot's wife?"

"She turned to salt."

I didn't know that one.

"What happened after the French Revolution?"

Freedom and liberty.

"Longstanding political turmoil and then Napoleon," Larry aped, probably right out of the textbook.

Alright, so maybe I hadn't aced the test. But I had plenty of time to ace the next one. It was just rote memorization, anyway. Besides, it's like, what happens when you get a good mark on a test? Absolutely nothing, that's what.

When I got home, it was only three o'clock. On my mother's insistence, I stared at some textbooks for a while before I got on my BMX and sped away to the Drophouse. I figured I'd see Joe and Eric there because they usually went right after school. And sure enough, there they were, right next to the easiest drop.

I decided to tease them a little. "Hey guys, don't break your neck staring down that drop."

"Well, why don't you do it?" Joe retorted.

"Nah, I'm good," I said, purely out of habit.

"Man, Jacob isn't gonna do a drop until his balls drop, yo," Eric said.

Joe lost it. He ran around Eric exclaiming, "Oh shiiet," and "What up," and "Bro." By the end, he was just shouting "Bro" over and over.

I was starting to remember why I didn't hang out with Eric any longer, and I decided to show him. Forcing the bike into first gear, I rammed that drop. For a second, I was suspended in the air in that wonderful bigger-than-life kind of way, but overall, it was the most anti-climactic thing I had done in my life. The drop was from a two-foot-high streak of dirt onto the ground. It was almost like riding your bike off the curb of a sidewalk, and I didn't even stick the landing or anything. Still, I totally flexed my bicep at the guys just to show off.

The rest of the guys came trickling in. All around the windmill, they circled around each other, dropping down from various heights. Sometimes sticking the landing and sometimes falling flat on the ground. But always jumping with the same ridiculous sense of purpose. The girls didn't show up until five o'clock, and I was there to greet them with crazy bravado, my hands in the air like a ringmaster or something. "Welcome to the drop house."

Joanne put her hands on her hips. "Yep, pretty gay."

I gave her this condescending smile she didn't know what to do with. Her mouth became a quiver looking for arrows and coming up short. I suppose she was used to people backing off quickly. Meanwhile, I gave Veronica the eye and had her blushing like a schoolgirl. "Who wants to see inside the windmill?"

"Whatever," Joanne said.

I led the girls past Larry's drop on the way inside, so-called because Larry was the only one who dared to jump it. The drop was from the highest patch of dirt, which arched down into the lowest hole and up again. Every moment Larry spent at the Drophouse he did that drop. He'd stick the landing every time, circle around, and do it again. By the time I had led my group into the windmill, I'd lost about half of it.

Eric and Joe were lounging on the first floor. It was musty and dark. Unlike the other floors, there were no windows down here. Strewn here and there over the floor were bags full of all the outer layers of corn, the husk of it; we used them as seats. I took the group right upstairs.

On the second floor were two imposing stone circles resting on top of one another. Attached to them was an intricate system of gradually larger gears leading to the top floor, a little nook we had designated for dates. Although in all the time we spent at the windmill, I don't think anyone brought a girl up there.

"Here is where they crush the corn."

"Duh," Joanne said.

I looked at my group to find the only ones left were Joanne, a couple of other girls and then that dunce Eric had joined us at some point. "Where did everyone go?"

I was walking to the stairs when Joanne stopped me. "So why did you bring me up here anyway?" Her eyes were a little slanted, and she was twirling her hair.

That was rich. She couldn't resist my charms. I grabbed her by the shoulders and moved her out of the way. "No, sweetheart."

Veronica was outside. She was watching Larry do his drop. Honestly? Larry was a schoolboy content to spend his days riding his bike, and she was practically drooling over this piss-ant. Well, if he could do it then I could. Eric's bike was to my right. I got on it, and as soon as Larry had dropped, I came after.

I was high in the air when I realized there might be some art to this biking thing. I saw the worn landing strip beneath me and felt my feet going gradually further from the pedals. As a last resort, I threw the bike away and let myself fall into the hole.

I stood up to one of the worst scenes the human experience offers: a group of high schoolers laughing at me. The only consolation was that Veronica was standing right there next to me. She was wearing a black leather jacket, white t-shirt, and those pink sweatpants that said "juicy" on the ass. Her hair was down, heavy makeup, annoyed.

"That was an epic fail," she said. I forgot that was a saying.

I didn't know how to respond. "I'm fine."

"You sure?"

"I am a little shook."

"What?"

"Never mind, come here." I grabbed her hand, and I didn't mind the group of high schoolers still laughing at me as we walked into the windmill. Joe gave me a cheeky little wink as I led Veronica up the stairs all the way to the top floor.

There were a couple of mats up there for lying down under all the gears and stuff. To the right of the stairs, you could look outside at the windmill sails. On the other end was a box with various junk, some from us, some from the owner. The scene was right out of one of those awful tween movies, so she must have been loving this. She looked deep into my eyes, but I couldn't tell what she thought because, to be honest, she always looked like she was going to slap me.

I sat on one mat and patted the empty space next to me. "Have a seat."

She crossed her arms. "First, you act all crazy on the phone, then you jump to your death, and now you've dragged me up here. What's up?"

I had this stupid smile on my face reaching up to my ears. "I just wanted to spend some time with you."

"Do you like me?"

"Of course, I like you. I'm up here with you, aren't I?"

"But why do you like me?"

I didn't have an answer. And she only gave me a second too.

"See, you can't even say," she said.

"I just like you. I can't explain it."

"But I screw everything up, and even though Joanne says I'm pretty, I still haven't lost my braces."

She had braces?

She tried to gesticulate, but she was all over the place, so it looked like she was swatting flies or something. "I'm no good at math, and I spend all my time on messenger."

I stood up and poked at the gears a little.

"What's this?" She pulled a magazine out of the box, and the centerfold spread out. It was Tori Black with one of her long legs all the way in the air and a devil's smile. Penthouse, December issue.

"Is this why you brought me here?"

"Well –"

She lay down on the mat and put her right leg as far up in the air as she could. Wasn't anything like how Tori did it, but I slid up next to her anyway; she really did have braces. All teasing like, I pinched her thigh a little, and she got her foot out of the air and nuzzled up against me.

I said, "See, I do like you."

She pulled her leather jacket down from her right shoulder.

I put my hand on her waist and moved it slowly up her t-shirt, but she pushed it away.

"Oh my god," she said.

My hands clenched of their own accord as she sat up and took off her leather jacket. She laid back down on her side. I put my hands on her waist again. I pushed her on her back and sort of laid on top of her.

"You're insane."

I was leaning in for a kiss when a flash of light made me self-aware.

Joanne had her phone up, taking pictures. "Got you." She ducked down.

I don't know if it was the flash of light, but I got a good look at myself in the moment and felt downright slimy. I wasn't supposed to be there. I was an adult. As I stood up, Veronica said, "What's the matter? We weren't doing anything wrong."

She hadn't been. I had meant to fix the past and ended up trying to fuck a teenager in a windmill.

"I have to go." As I stumbled down this ruin of a windmill, I had a lot of trouble imagining myself there for the next two years. I wanted the thing torn down right there and then. Joanne was showing everyone her pictures. The girls giggled, and the guys made encouraging but offensive gestures. I wasn't supposed to be there. After frantically looking for my bike, I sped away. I biked past the auto shop and the pub and ended up at home.

My mother was making a mess of the bathroom, all her make-up strewn across the sink, as I darted past her into my bedroom. I got a sudden urge to throw out everything in there. Got one of those big black trash bags and chucked my plant in there. Swept all the crap out from under the bed and sorted it.

"Hey there, kid." It was my old man. He had bags under his eyes, and his jacket was torn in two places. I didn't remember him that way.

"Well, aren't you going to give your old man a hug?" He stepped toward me.

I put up my fists, but he just moved them aside and gave me this strangulation of a hug. He smelled like when you leave a beer open overnight. "Gotta work up some muscle, or else you have to hug me."

Thing is, I already had gotten a lot stronger. And the last time he came around, I kicked him out the door.

"Just you wait," I said.

He let out a seemingly endless guffaw that eventually turned into a coughing fit. "Come on, we're just fooling around. Like the good old days."

I was fuming. "Fuck that. We never had any good old days. It's a disgusting lie you tell yourself to justify what you are now."

He looked like he was about to jump me. But the words just came out, like throw-up. I continued, "Because if you were ever good, then it's possible there's a kernel of good inside, beneath all the outer layers of shit."

"Relax," he said.

"But there is nothing good underneath, it's all husk." I was reminded of the bags at the bottom of the windmill left behind after the old looney's failed enterprise as I put my finger to my father's chest. "You're husk."

He knocked me out with one punch.

When I came to, it was six AM. The date was right there on the alarm clock, but I could have cared less. I got up right away and walked into the bathroom to take a long look at myself in the mirror. Suppose I hadn't done that in a while, not properly, at least. Thing is, I'd get stuck at a certain point looking at myself in the mirror, where I'd get nauseous and have a little case of vertigo, so I couldn't stand properly. Not because of my haircut, or my shitty facial symmetry, although that stuff didn't help. It was more that I really saw me, past and present. Or that I saw what everyone else saw when they looked at me. I forced myself through it, staring myself down, and figured I should brush my teeth.

Once I'd brushed my teeth, I ate a proper breakfast: a plate of fried eggs, bacon, and an avocado; people keep telling me that shit is good for you. I gathered up all the dirty laundry and got pretty far along with the trash before I had to start my day. When I stepped outside, the sun was coming up from behind a distant mountain.

The Greenest Initiative

"We're putting a green initiative in place," the new manager said.

Eveline stared outside the break room window. After pretending to be interested in the first few seemingly random changes that Cecilia had made since being transferred there, she learned that it was enough to answer in the affirmative after the meeting. In the meantime, she watched a piece of greenery burrow its way through the pavement in the parking lot. It had nowhere to go, no ecosystem to be part of in the hard cement lot. Yet it struggled upwards all the same, defiant in the face of purpose and belonging.

Next to Eveline, bathed in fluorescent

light, the two older women who worked with her were listening intently to their new manager. The weekly meeting was one of the few times that Eveline met her co-workers, as Eveline was in charge of the calls, and they dealt strictly with the archives. One of them was called Kate, and the other Julia. But it was anyone's guess which was which. Eveline suspected they would make a great case study for someone figuring out the influence of one's environment since the two women had probably kept synchronous routines for years now.

"Don't worry, this won't interfere with the other changes, like making this place more productive," Cecilia said. "Are you guys excited?"

"Yes," Eveline lied.

"Wonderful. Meeting concluded."

Eveline counted the steps back to her desk. Eight. The break room was right next to the lobby, where Eveline sat. Depending on the briskness of her steps, it was only six steps to her desk, but sometimes as much as nine. Roughly seven plus or minus two. The same as the number of items a person can remember at once. Eveline wondered if you could contain a person's life within that number. Number of close friends: five. Shows you watch on repeat: eight.

The phone rang.

"Where do I renew my driver's license?" said a man with a raspy voice.

Eveline drew a vertical line on a piece of paper next to that exact sentence. It was a piece of paper with seven questions written on it, titled "FAQ OFF."

"The DMV," Eveline said.

Eveline worked in a government-run information center, which basically meant people called her when they didn't know where else to call. It was all super basic information that anyone should know, and usually, people asked one of the questions she had memorized the answers to in the first week; in the worst-case scenario, she had to google something. Not once had she consulted the moldy papers behind her, known as "the archive." The old ladies from upstairs would go in there with a stack of papers, and just before Eveline filled out a missing papers report, they would emerge with an entirely different stack of papers.

After the call, Eveline stared at the sofa on the other side of the room. You could come in and ask your questions in person;

there were even some magazines that Eveline had read three times each. But the only time anyone came was when a homeless guy took a nap on the couch, and they had to call the police. The smell lingered for a whole week.

Eveline turned on a jazz playlist and drew the banana she planned to have for a late-morning snack. She liked jazz, but more than that, she liked being someone who likes jazz. She couldn't name a single song on the playlist that Spotify had put together for her. But the way it continuously hit you across the head with blue notes and constant improvisation made it perfect background music when she was drawing. The best songs made her unconsciously tap her index finger on her left hand against her thumb.

When she was satisfied with her drawing, she put it next to the FAQ OFF, ate the banana and threw the peel in the bin under her desk. Then, she emailed the Sustainability Mandate Upholding Group, stating that her workplace would participate in the Green Initiative, thus completing the first step of the initiative. That called for a break, and she played Minesweeper for about half an hour.

That distinct sound made by two wobbly wheels and hard plastic lids banging against plastic filled the lobby as Cecilia dragged in two large bins marked "Plastic" and "Paper." "We're going to recycle," she said.

Eveline looked under her desk, where the small trash can held the peel off her banana and a couple of crumpled-up pieces of paper. She looked back at Cecilia and formed her lower lip into something resembling a smile.

"Aren't you excited?" Cecilia said.

"Yes."

Before Eveline had uttered that one syllable, Cecilia was already heading back outside. "Just you wait," she said on her way.

Eveline stood up and checked out the bins. They were like the ones in her apartment building. She never knew what to do with the stuff that had both plastic and paper in it, like those pastry boxes with plastic film so you can see it before you buy it. She figured the people who took the bins knew what to do with it.

Cecilia came back with another set of bins. Metal and organic waste. "Look at these beauties."

"Yeah… they're beauties, alright."

"From here on out, every piece of trash goes into these bins."

"Yes." Eveline reached under her desk and sorted the three pieces of trash into the bins.

"Huh, that's it?" Cecilia frowned.

"It's still early."

"Right."

Cecilia moved to Eveline's desk in the way that hyper-productive people sometimes do: not exactly rushed but not leaving any breathing space between actions either. Before Eveline could say anything she was sifting through the papers on the desk. She pushed Eveline's drawing to the side.

"What are you looking for?"

"Trash."

Eveline grabbed her drawing and held it close to her chest. Could Cecilia distinguish between art and recyclables?

"Hmm." Cecilia picked up the FAQ OFF, held it against the fluorescent lights and peered at each individual item. An expressly capitalist look glinted in her eyes. "Are these questions from the callers?"

Eveline tapped her thumb and forefinger together in the rhythm of "So What" by

Miles Davis. "I figured I should keep track of the most asked questions."

"These are fantastic," Cecelia said. And she repeated the phrase to herself more than anything as she strolled back into her office. When Cecilia was gone, Eveline hid her banana sketch in a drawer and went back to pretending to work.

The next day, as she sat down to clock herself in, she noticed that her phone had been replaced. When it hadn't rung once by lunchtime, Eveline rapped on Cecilia's office door.

"Come in."

Eveline stepped into the office, which was full of cabinets and strewn about papers. A streak of light shone through the blinds, dividing Cecilia into rectangular segments as she hunched over a large chunk of paperwork. Eveline would have never guessed there was so much paperwork associated with this place. It was enough to fill the bin in the lobby twice over.

"Did you replace my phone?" Eveline said. "It isn't working."

Cecilia looked up from her work. "Should be fine, I tried it yesterday."

"It hasn't rung all morning."

She waved the question away. "That's probably because of the answering machine. It's redirecting the calls based on you FAQ."

"Redirecting the calls?"

"Yes, I noticed most of the questions you get have to do with other departments. Now you'll only get the questions that no one else can answer. I estimate this will increase productivity by upwards of forty percent."

"Alright." Eveline staggered back to the lobby.

The new phone still had a plastic sheet covering its panel. She peeled it from the upper right corner, careful to uncover the top line of digits before she moved on down. Then she stood up and sorted the film into the bin for plastic. Back to her desk. She felt herself sink into the chair. The room was horribly silent. There wasn't even the prospect of anything meaningful to do.

She opened Evergreen University's website and then immediately exited it. Somewhere on that website, under the art department tab, was her half-finished application. She had already put in the samples of her work. All that was left was to put in some personal information and hit submit. Every week she would open up the website without doing it. Just like how she was supposed to sweep the lobby every week and didn't ever do that either.

The feather duster was in the bottom desk drawer, and Eveline swept away like it was literally her only purpose in life. She took ten minutes to sweep every surface in the lobby. The railing on the stairs to the old ladies was dusty, and Eveline worked her way upstairs. She wondered if the old ladies' office was the same as her first day when Kate showed her the building, and to her astonishment, it seemed even the blinds were pulled up to the same level. Neither lady looked up when she entered, preferring to tap away at full pace, one finger at a time.

"Hey, guys," Eveline said.

"Good morning," Kate said.

"I just found some free time in my schedule. Is there something I can do to help you guys?"

Julie lifted her gaze to Eveline and peered as if they were trying to find figures on Eveline's face and finding only bumps and irregularities.

"Eveline. Yes, I've just found a mistake in our files. It's urgent that it gets fixed. You know how to work the registry editor, right?"

Urgent. Eveline had never heard the word uttered in the office. "Yes. I even learned the keyboard shortcuts."

Kate stared at Eveline with that same blank stare, and Eveline regretted mentioning the shortcuts she never needed to use. Kate stood up and handed Eveline a stack of folders. It wobbled in her arms, but for an urgent stack of folders, it was rather dusty.

"These files have all been categorized under Clause 17-b, when, in fact, they should have been categorized under Clause 17-d."

Julia chuckled. "What a silly mistake. Would you be a dear and fix it?"

Eveline hesitated to ask what would happen if the files remained under Clause 17-b. Maybe someone would lose their house, or there would be a resurgence of Nazis. Probably not, but Eveline never really understood why there were Nazis, and it would be nice if there were some measures in place to stop them. Preferably ones operated by people smarter than herself.

"Sure thing," she said.

Back at her desk, she diligently looked up each file in the registry and changed the category from 17-b to 17-d. It was a time-con-suming task, as even though all the files were under 17-b, there was no way to get a clear overview of them all, nor was it possible to change the registration for multiple files at a time. In all her urgency, she hadn't even leafed through a single file until she finished a whole folder's worth. In bold serif letters, the title on the folder read, "Registry of Dog Owners in the South Side of City, 1986-1995." She put it aside and started dusting some more.

There must have been some point to all these files and paperwork. If not the stack she had been given, then something in the archives. She had never been back there, but the phone wasn't going to ring, so she might as well. A part of her always assumed most of this stuff served a purpose that was be-yond her and could only be seen from the lofty heights of parliament. But maybe she only assumed that so she wouldn't have to worry about it.

The light flickered above her as Eveline leafed through files. City council meeting at-tendance records, overview of unpaid parking tickets of the deceased, blueprints for buildings commissioned but never built.

It was a maze full of rubbish and registries scattered over busted-up shelving racks. No Minotaur, no dragons, no treasure.

She ran her finger across an empty shelf. It was covered in dust. Maybe all the juicy stuff was in the back. All the rest of it was a lot of noise, hiding the scarlet letter from whistle-blowers or something. Trying her theory, Eveline cut the corner and bumped into something on the floor.

"Shit," she muttered.

It was a shredder. One of those little portable ones you can have at home. Was that what they did back here? Took all the incriminating stuff and shredded it? Eveline gathered a few strips of paper and put them next to one another, but she couldn't make anything out. Maybe there wasn't anything remotely interesting in the whole building. Maybe those strips of paper were shredded because they were so uninteresting that not even the old ladies upstairs cared to keep them.

Eveline would have liked most of all to strut to her desk and draft a letter of resignation. If only someone had a question that didn't have to do with the DMV or taxes. Like how long you can keep your fake teeth in the sun before they go bad or whether the President of France has an official Twitter account. At least that way, there would have been a point to her coming in today.

She sat down on the shredder and buried her face in her hands. She should have been in some liberal arts schoolhouse party, drunkenly slurring about the way Picasso had influenced the modern psyche, eventually taking some dweeb back to her dorm where she had amassed stacks of paintings she could pretend were going to be revolutionary one day and use feminist rhetoric to convince the dweeb to let her finger him in the ass.

And then the phone rang. She followed the ringtone back to her desk and picked up the phone.

"Hello."

"How do you know if you're really alive?"

"What?"

"Like, if you're really living life to its full potential or whatever."

Eveline opened google on her computer, but she didn't know what to type. She could hear indistinct noises on the other end of the line. Like someone was arguing or stifling a laugh. "Is this a prank call or something?"

"No, not a prank call. I really want to know."

"Well, I don't know," Eveline said through gritted teeth.

Again, Eveline heard muffled noises, tactlessly discussing her answer. "Are you going to ask an actual question?" she said.

"Sorry, I'm being rude." He coughed a deep and grating cough. "Do you know someone that knows the answer?"

"No, I don't." She paused. "I don't think anyone has the answer."

"That's alright. Thanks anyway." He hung up.

Eveline laid down the phone, gripped the handles of her chair and breathed deeply. Then she found her application to Evergreen University, filled out the remaining information in a frenzy and submitted it. The phone didn't ring for the rest of the day, but Eveline didn't care.

In the next few weeks, Cecilia put more initiatives in place. "The Save Coffee Initiative," which meant that you should ask if other people were having coffee before brewing a fresh batch after three in the afternoon. She put up a poster in the bathroom detailing how to wash your hands in case you were going to perform open heart surgery in the next five minutes, which didn't seem particularly green, but Eveline didn't follow the instructions anyway. And somehow Cecilia added two more bins to the line-up, but they were all moved to a newly built storage area at the back of the building, so Eveline never knew what went into them. Apparently, this constituted the second phase of the Green Initiative.

Eveline kept practicing her shading and double-point perspectives. She was made to shred the documents already digitized. They were only keeping the absolutely most im-portant documents, which apparently meant those that were specific to this geographical area and kept by no one else. But even those were being shipped to another location. One day she looked behind her and saw an empty space where the archives had been. It was surprisingly small.

The water cooler went away. So did the magazines and the couch. It wasn't very green to keep resources that weren't really being used. At some point during all of this, they had completed the third phase. The bathroom got motion sensor lights on a timer, so Eveline had to reach up and wave her hands every twenty seconds. Eventually, Eveline sat in an empty room, wondering whether the other people in the building could possibly be doing any work.

When she got her acceptance letter to Evergreen, she brought it to work, eager to show everyone. She skipped through her usual route, gleefully aware that in a short while, she would take it for the last time. Upon arrival, she found that the lot was walled off by a metal fence and that the building had been bulldozed.

Taped to the metal fence was a piece of paper with the city stamp on which it stood "This workplace has completed the fourth phase of the Green Initiative."

The Mumbler

"Some children simply obtain a disposition that doesn't allow for a lot of human interactions," Ian said to Henry's parents.

Henry Vogler's disposition had manifested itself in such a way as to make him mumble every syllable. That is not to say he wouldn't interact with people. He could make himself fairly understood with a combination of mumbles and hand gestures, but his speech itself was entirely incoherent. When he turned thirteen, his parents finally admitted that the problem wasn't going to solve itself and hired a speech therapist to work with Henry over the summer break.

"Could you tell me anything about

Henry that I might use to get his attention?" Ian said.

"He spends most of his time at home in our library. He doesn't care about the television, but he loves books," Mr. Vogler said. "I don't even know if he understands what he reads, but you might start with that."

But Henry wouldn't talk (or mumble) to his therapist at all. He thought Ian was pretentious. The only times Henry reacted at all was when his mother came into the living room to bring him pastries. His favorite was the Berliner, which, if one was less than discreet, one could have likened to Henry. Ian forbade the rotund pastries until Henry would cooperate. This did not make Henry any more appreciative of Ian, but it made him cooperative.

Ian came every weekday and sat with Henry for three hours. During their sessions, they would sit opposite one another on separate leather sofas. Ian would read a passage from a book in the Voglers' living room bookcase – which wasn't as large as the ones in the home library but still respectable – and Henry would repeat it. Ian tried to appeal to Henry with the likes of *Romeo and Juliet* or the Brownings, but Henry liked *Titus*

Andronicus better. In time, Henry became articulate; he became eloquent. He learned how best to put stress on words, where to emphasize them, and how to speak clearly and calmly. His voice became butter. Listening to him was like listening to an experienced radio personality. When the summer ended, stepping out of their door, Ian pronounced to the Voglers that Henry would be "the most popular kid in class, solely because of his voice."

But on the first day of school, Henry didn't make much use of his voice. As usual, he sat in the back of the classroom and didn't speak unless spoken to. When no one in class knew the definition of tyranny, the teacher jokingly tried her luck with Henry. Everyone was aghast not only that he answered the question but at the eloquence of his answer: "Tyranny is any callous, senseless, or arbitrary use of power."

The impact of his reply became evident during recess when a number of the children crowded him, each talking over the other: "You can talk now? Guys, the Mumbler can talk. How did you know that answer? Have you always been smart?"

Henry couldn't shake them. "You imbeciles have no idea how smart I am, and it would take me hours to explain. Now leave me alone."

One of the larger kids, the sort that nature seems to place outside of convenience stores, overheard Henry's retort. He walked up to Henry, looked him in the eye, and punched him in the gut. Henry collapsed on the ground and didn't stand up until everyone had dispersed.

He did not return to class, nor did he go home. He went to the bakery. He had a habit of going there after school, where he provided the staff with magnificent displays of gluttony. They were always delighted to have him. Besides having a liberal allowance, he was easy to please – just give him whatever he pointed at. When he entered, all three staff members (and both of the customers) turned. The freshly baked pastries were all trying to outdo the others in terms of fragrance. Behind the counter stood the head baker, a stout woman who always put her hands on her hips before talking.

"Why aren't you at school?"

Henry all but ignored her and plumped his finger on the glass. "Can I have the biggest, fattest Berliner? The one that looks like you." He held his finger on the glass as everyone went silent.

The head baker lifted her hands from her sides and placed them on the display counter. "What did you just say to me?"

He lowered his finger. What was wrong? This was how he always ordered Berliners. Why was she not wrapping up his Berliner? "I ordered a pastry," he said.

"You aren't getting anything until you learn to shut your goddamn mouth."

Henry's face impersonated an Edvard Munch painting – you know which one. He looked around for help, but everyone was mimicking his expression. He turned and walked out of the store. From there, he went no more than ten meters before dropping onto a bench.

What had happened? He was aware that most people disliked him, but they never punched him or threw him out of stores. It wasn't as if he had changed, really; he had said the same sort of things as every other day. Was it how he said it? Was there something in his manner or tone that displeased people? It must be. There must be some antagonizing quality to his voice. But Ian said they would like his voice. So maybe they were jealous instead. Either way, he had a solution – he would stop speaking.

Henry's resolve delighted him. He jumped off the bench and imitated zipping his mouth shut. From now on, he would have to act out everything, so there could be no sparing theatrics. He did his best silly walk on the way home, where he would spread the moving leg outward, dangle it a little, and plonk it on the ground. Everyone who passed him smiled, and some even did their own silly walk. When he stopped talking people were fond of him, even more so than when he had mumbled.

Once he reached his house, he walked normally up the stairs leading to the front door. The air inside was overbearing. Still hungry, Henry made for the kitchen, only to come across his father slouched over a typewriter in the living room.

"You should be at school."

Henry was silent.

"You aren't going to answer me?"

Henry mimed zipping his mouth.

"You've stopped talking already." Henry's father rubbed the bridge of his nose. "After all the trouble we've gone through with Ian. You know, we damn near give you anything you could want, and this is what we get in return: a fucking mime."

Henry looked down at his feet and waited for the barrage to stop. Mr. Vogler's yelling brought Henry's mother in from the kitchen. Between yelling back at his father, she offered Henry many remedies: a G.I. Joe figure, pastries, love. Henry was silent. It seemed his resolve had changed nothing here. They kept arguing, and it was a while before his father addressed him.

"If you are so determined to disobey us at every turn, then why don't you just leave?"

The idea struck Henry. He could just leave. He turned from his parents and climbed the stairs to the sound of "Where do you think you're going?" and, "Oh, let him go." Once in his room, he packed a leather duffle bag. He owned a suitcase, but he thought the duffle bag was more appropriate for running away. He was sensible enough to pack a set of clothes, nonsensical enough to pack a few books, and greedy to pack a day-old pastry. He figured he would go to the city. He had heard people were less engaging there; you could walk through the whole thing, and no one would so much as greet you. You were meant to be silent.

He walked downstairs and looked at his parents. Where anyone else would have said his goodbyes and possibly told their parents off, Henry just waved; they didn't notice. He started walking silly as soon as he was outside.

II

Henry knocked on the door of a farm and took one step back. He stood between two Doric pilasters holding the outlines of a pediment, almost like on a courthouse. So, the main building wasn't necessarily very farm like, but the rest of them were red barns and weathered cottages. There was a garden behind the main building whose trees reached far above it; the garden was separated from farmland by a hedge.

It probably hadn't been a good idea to walk to the city.

The door opened to a man wearing a white t-shirt and dirty overalls. He was large enough to fill the entire doorway. Henry could have sworn the man's hand left a mark on the door handle. Neither of them said anything until Henry coughed and kicked his duffle bag lightly toward the open door.

"Hello," the man said.

Henry lowered his head and cast his eyes up toward the stranger, making himself look pathetic to solicit some sympathy from the man.

"What do you want?" the man said.

Henry clasped his hands together in a begging motion.

"Are you looking for work?"

Henry shook his head violently.

The man kicked the duffle bag toward Henry. "We aren't taking freeloaders. We do have room for another farmhand."

Henry looked toward the now dimly lit road, but he couldn't see another house in either direction. He nodded his head reluctantly, picked up his duffle bag, and tried to shuffle past the man, who stopped Henry and shook his hand.

"The name's Mr. Smith. You must be hungry."

Mr. Smith guided Henry by putting his hand around him, effectively funneling Henry into the kitchen. After feeding him some reheated casserole in the kitchen, Mr. Smith showed Henry into the worker's sleeping quarters. It was one of the red cottages, on the left side of the main building. Inside were seven beds all stacked up to one wall, six of whom were occupied, and at the opposite wall was a trunk for each bed. On the far end was a sink and mirror. The duffle bag went in the trunk and Henry fell asleep instantly.

He woke in an empty cottage. The first thing he did was wash his face, which was quite the task since he couldn't see his reflection properly in the dirty mirror. Then he opened his duffle bag. The last pastry was so stale he had confused it with his books while rummaging through the bag; only for emergencies, he thought. As he sat down to read, a bell rang in the main building. Must be lunchtime. But when he stepped out of the cottage, everyone was walking toward him. The workers, all of whom were at and around his age, walked past him to the field, but his landlord came toward him.

"Look who slept in. You missed lunch."

Henry shrugged his shoulders, even though he was hungry.

Mr. Smith led Henry to the fields where another kid was charged with training him. The kid must have been only a couple of years older than Henry, but he was much taller and broader and seemed perfectly at ease, even though he had a twenty-kilo bag of fertilizer slung over one shoulder.

He gave Henry a pat on the shoulder and said, "Hey there, I'm Sikes. Is Mr. Smith giving you any grief?"

Henry shook his head and got to work.

He never imagined potato farming would be fun, but he didn't realize he'd be bad at it. It was simple in principle: plough this, pick that, move this, shovel, sweat. But he was slow to it, and it would be generous to say he did half the work of anyone else.

At the end of the day, they all shuffled into the dining room in the main building. Mr. Smith gave everyone two scoops of goulash, but when he came to Henry, he looked him up and down and gave him one scoop.

Sikes snagged Henry's bread. "So, he is giving you grief."

When they got back to their cottage, Henry found that his bed was on the other side of the wall from everyone else's. He wouldn't have had the energy to move it back, even if he had the guts. Henry had never been so hungry in his life, and when the other boys had fallen asleep, he ate his last pastry, even though it cut his gums.

The next day Henry woke up with everyone else. This earned him three half-meals. After work, in the cottage, all the other boys were horsing around as Henry tried to read in his bed. They called each other dope, or kike, or faggot, as they felt appropriate. They pushed each other, jumped between the beds, and periodically they ganged up on no one in particular, just to see if he could stand it.

Henry had read the same page three times when Sikes walked up to him and said, "What do we call this one?"

"The Monk," said one of the smaller kids. "Because he doesn't talk."

"That's good," said Sikes, "because he doesn't do much either."

Henry burrowed his head into his book and mumbled, "At least I know how to read, you damn imbeciles."

Sikes said. "So, you can talk. I mean, you can mumble at least. That's what we'll call you: the Mumbler."

Henry threw down his book and stormed out. They called after him, "The Mumbler, look at the Mumbler go." He ran straight forward through an opening in the hedge and before he knew it he was in the garden behind the main building. Vines of wisteria surrounded the path and occasionally brushed up against his face as he went farther into the garden. The birch trees reached high in the air, creating domes here and there. In the middle of the garden was a statue.

He couldn't hear the boys anymore, so he stopped to look at the statue. It was of a mostly naked guy grabbing a mostly naked girl; although, it looked like he was running, so maybe he was chasing her. She was doing something else entirely. She was throwing her hands in the air, but her fingers were twigs, and so was part of her hair. The whole scene was strange, but he couldn't look away.

As Henry admired the statue, a figure appeared on the balcony. She was around his age, wearing a purple shift dress. She stroked the edges of a handheld mirror with a metallic garland. Henry walked closer, half hidden by the wisteria. She was like the moon or maybe the sun. However beautiful girls were usually symbolized, she was ex- actly that. He wished he could be her mirror. She lifted her eyes from her reflection and sighed. Henry stepped into view, hoping she would see him, hoping she would speak. He stepped on a twig as he moved.

"Hello?" she said. "Is someone there? Where are you? Hello."

It must have been too dark for her to

spot him. He would have to speak, even though it meant breaking his resolve. As for what to say, it just came to him.

"I am called Henry, but if that name does not please you, I will be whatever –"

"You're kind of fat."

"Uh, I swear by the moon –"

She brought the mirror to her face and walked inside the house. "Whatever."

Henry stood still for a long moment. He must have done something wrong. This wasn't how it had happened in the stories. He bowed his head about as much as he could and walked back to the cottage in that fashion.

Henry came back every day to woo her in grand paraphrased soliloquies. He told her how he loved her, and then he counted the ways: I love you in the breadth times length times height, where my soul can reach, though sometimes out of sight. I love you freely, purely, and with passion put to use. I stand in my old briefs I wear with childhood faith. I love you with blood and sweat and tears, and if alright by God, I'll love you though you're dead.

She always showed him that same dismissive attitude. After a week, he gave up and grew despondent. He never improved his work but contented himself with his half-meals instead; sometimes, he wouldn't finish those either. He never moved his bed, and he didn't talk to anyone. When he got his half-pay, he stowed it in his duffle bag, and when the other boys went into town to spend theirs, he stayed behind. When he had gotten one full paycheck in whole, he did the same. After work, he read in a nook in the garden and would occasionally catch glimpses of her.

He thought about leaving, but the thought of her stopped him. One afternoon, as he slid past the Ionic column holding the balcony, he saw her standing next to the path admiring a branch of wisteria, and when he tried to sneak past her, she called out to him, "Hi there."

He turned toward her, shoulders stooped, eyes down. "Hi."

"Are you one of the new workers? You all seem to come and go so fast."

She didn't recognize him. He dared to

look at her and noticed that she didn't look at him the same way – as if he was really standing somewhere further back. Now her look was a little downward and a little forward at the same time. Henry was baffled. He looked himself over for the first time in two months and found that he had lost his flab. He was slim going on toned, if a little emaciated.

"I'm Rarity," she said. "What's your name? Are you really working here?"

"Henry, and yes I –"

"You talk funny."

Henry stopped in his tracks.

With a smile on her face, she took him by his sweaty hand and led him inside, through the sitting room, the grand foyer, up the grand staircase, and into her room. It was pink from top to bottom, with its own private bathroom. Her bed was covered in pillows and her makeup table was covered in jewelry.

"Well, you don't have to work anymore. You can sleep in one of the guest rooms and you can hang out with me. Put this on, won't you?" She handed him a two-button single-breasted suit with an orchid boutonniere.

"I guess I have been wearing the same outfit for a while."

"We can go shopping in the city, and take pictures, and…"

Henry went into the bathroom to change. "I've always wanted to go to the city," he said.

"…we can eat good food and go dancing." When Henry presented himself, Rarity unbuttoned his lower button and handed him her mirror. "Hold this, will you?"

She sat on the mountain of pillows propped up against the headboard, while he sat on the far end of the bed, pointing the mirror at her.

"How is my hair," she said, "do you like my jewelry?"

"You're very pretty –"

"I have a lot of jewelry. Daddy buys it for me." She jumped out of bed, got a jewelry box from her dresser, and sat down in the exact same spot, in the exact same pose. Then she tried on every single piece of jewelry in that box, recounting how she had gotten each one.

"Daddy bought this one for my birthday. And this one I got on this boring family trip, I really had to work for it."

Henry had been estimating how long he would have to hold the mirror by counting the remaining pieces of jewelry when she closed the box and got a new one. It was dark when she finished the second box, and Henry had both hands on the mirror.

"I'm tired," she said.

"You're tired? I've sat here holding this mirror for –"

"You can go now. Just find one of the guest rooms and sleep in there."

Henry stomped out of the room and slammed the door behind him. Well, he sort of slammed it; it was hard enough to make a statement, probably – it was ambiguous. He considered opening the door just to slam it again but decided not to. He was annoyed, but he couldn't quite tell why. Was Rarity not as pretty as he had thought? No, she was pretty alright. He figured he would do as she said and figure it out later; then, he could fix it. Maybe it was something about him. If it was something about him, then Rarity could fix it.

He started opening doors. Bathroom. Library. Study. Mr. Smith's study – with Mr. Smith in it. He was hunched over the table, wearing a suit, dealing with some papers, but what struck Henry were his reading glasses. They seemed so out of place on Mr. Smith's precipitous face that Henry burst out laughing the moment he walked in. Mr. Smith's face became as if it was filled to the brim with some burning liquid. He marched to Henry, "What are you doing up here, and what's so goddamn funny."

Henry gathered himself for the most part. "I was in your daughter's room. And you look really stupid with glasses."

Henry stopped laughing when Mr. Smith grabbed him by the neck and dragged him outside. Henry was still struggling when they went down the stairs, and Mr. Smith opened the door. By the time they were inside the workers' quarters, Henry was limp. In one movement, with one hand on Henry's neck, Mr. Smith threw the displaced bed into place and chucked Henry's duffle bag at him; he startled the entire workforce. Mr. Smith then took Henry outside, threw him into the Bentley, and tasked the butler to drive him to the bus station in town. Once there, Henry was encouraged to take the late bus to the city, and he did. It wasn't until the bus had left that the butler noticed the missing posters with Henry's face on them.

III.

The first thing Henry noticed about the city wasn't the towering skyscrapers or the sea of people; it was the sounds. The conjoined rattle of footsteps, honking of horns, and revving of engines made the hubbub accompaniment to the talking. Henry hadn't realized there would be so much talking. But, he was quick to note that talking was reserved to the coffee shops, angry taxi drivers, or the stores – where only the teller and the customer would talk while the rest stood and waited. As long as he stuck to the sidewalk, he was exempt from talking. In any case, he wasn't particularly inclined to talk after his conversation with Mr. Smith.

So, he walked. He walked past statues of great founders, great fountains, and the great powerhouses of artistic merit: opera houses, libraries, museums. He walked until his feet hurt and his stomach churned. Then he stood in a taciturn line, and when it was his turn, he pointed to a revolving pizza, laid the exact price on the table and ate.

As he continued his tour of the city, the light shifted from clear sunlight to the artificial yellowy white of the streetlamps, and

Henry searched for somewhere to stay. The first hotel he found was an ancient beige, with superfluous pilasters and flowery capitals. He walked through the lobby, up to the reception and pointed to the keys behind the receptionist, who wasn't much older than Henry.

"Good evening," the receptionist said.

Henry laid a little money on the table.

"Do you want a room? If so, I'm going to need your name."

Henry hesitated.

"I have to put something."

Henry looked around the room. It couldn't lead to much harm if he spoke just once. "Henry."

The receptionist lifted his brows. "It's – for the night and you're in room number –." He pushed a key along the table.

Henry nodded, grabbed his key, and walked toward the elevator. As he waited for the elevator, a man wearing green bell bottoms, an orange shirt, and a purple suit approached him.

"Hey kid, nice suit." The man stretched his hand toward Henry." The name's Tom."

Henry pressed the elevator button one more time.

"You don't wanna talk to me?"

The elevator arrived, and Henry got on. Tom did not follow, but he watched Henry until the door closed. Henry went to his room and fell asleep reading *The Tables Turned*.

Unfortunately for Henry, it was almost as if Tom lived in the reception because every time Henry went in or out of the hotel, whether to read in the library or eat pizza, Tom was there to meet him. He walked alongside Henry from the entrance to the elevator, all the while bombarding him with questions. "What, are you a monk or something? That's fly and all, but can't you say something for me?"

At the end of the week, the receptionist called Henry over.

"Hey kid, um, sir. I need to know if you're gonna be staying any longer."

Henry sighed. Why wouldn't they leave him alone? He stormed to the reception, head held low. With Tom at his heels, he decided on his next move because it was powerful and it would keep him from having to talk. He slammed all of his remaining money on the table and waited for his change.

"This isn't enough to cover your stay so far."

Henry gasped, despite himself. Tom sprung into laughter. The receptionist started coming up with solutions – "Do you have any more money? Is there anyone who can pay for you?" But Henry just stood in place, unsure of what to do next.

Tom stopped laughing and said, "I'll pay your tab if you just talk a little for me."

Henry broke. "Fine, what do you want me to say?"

A couple of heads turned in the reception, and Tom turned a couple more when he started. "Yes, that's it; that magnificent voice. Kid, I work for KGBE, the radio station. I'm going to make you a star. And I'll get you your own room."

Henry needed somewhere to stay. "Ok," he said.

"Great!" Tom put his hand around Henry and pulled him along. "You'll love the radio host life. It's a life of luxury. What do you like? Candy? You'll be buying out candy stores in no time when you're a radio host. Don't worry about your stuff, we'll send somebody for it."

Before Henry knew it, he was sitting in a

recording studio with a contract on his lap. He sat next to the glass separating him from the control room where Tom was arguing with his colleague Richard. A grand piano in the far corner was easily ten meters away from him. Sheet music stands were scattered all over the place, and the ceiling, some thirty meters high, held tens of dangling lights. Henry could hear everything Tom and Richard said.

"We just got a brand new eight-track recorder, and you want to do talk radio with a child?" Richard said.

"I know it sounds crazy. But you should hear this kid talk, man. It's far out." Tom said.

"That doesn't mean he can conduct interviews."

"We can teach him."

"We don't have the setup."

"All we need is a table and a couple of chairs."

"We'd need to set up a profanity delay."

"No, we don't… like, what's the worst thing he could say?"

Tom went to turn on the PA when he noticed it had been on all along. "Shit.

Umm, hey kid, did you get a chance to look at the contract yet?"

Henry had read two pages of the twenty-page contract, and so far, he understood nothing. "Yes."

"That's great. Are you ready to sign?"

"Yes," Henry said.

Tom gave him a thumbs-up behind the glass, and the two men came into the recording room. Tom pulled a sheet music stand over, put the contract on it and handed Henry a pen. "So, mostly, we're gonna need you to conduct a series of interviews. That doesn't sound too hard, does it?"

Henry shook his head. He signed in large, wobbly capital letters. When he finished, Richard grabbed the contract and took it into the control room. Tom handed Henry a little wad of cash. "That's your allowance." Henry put it into his pocket without counting it. He was happy to be back on an allowance.

"Follow me," Tom said.

They went into the lobby, where Tom opened the door to the left; it was one of two doors in the lobby – the other was marked "control room." The door led them to a hallway. On the left was a single toilet, and at the end, there was a narrow stairway. The stairway led them into a bright room the size of the entire lower floor except for the recording room. It was furnished with a bed, table, sofa, bookcase, excessively colorful rug, acoustic guitar, upright piano. There were two windows, one was plain and overlooked the recording room, and the other was a round stained-glass window that almost filled the massive triangle that was the roof.

"This is the old control room," Tom said. "When we moved it downstairs, this became our party pad. You'll be staying here."

Henry stared up at the stained-glass window. There were figures between the colors.

"Oh yeah," Tom said. "This used to be a church. We got a good deal on it, too."

Henry sat down on the sofa and tested the springs a little. "Okay."

Tom looked around the room while nodding his head. He looked proud. "Oh, yeah, I have to get your stuff from the hotel. You just make yourself at home."

Henry went to sleep as soon as he left. When the light from the stained-glass window woke Henry, his duffle bag was next to the stairs. He walked straight downstairs to the recording room. Someone had set up a table with a microphone and a glass of water on each side, with some papers on the side closest to Henry.

"That's your seat."

Henry turned to find Richard in the control room.

"Tom isn't in today," Richard said. "He's probably hanging out in some lobby somewhere. I'm guessing that's how he found you."

Henry nodded.

"You could do with talking some more if you're going to be a radio show host. You will be interviewing someone from city council today. His information is on those papers."

Henry sat down in his chair. The papers had two handwritings. One was in neat rows, while the other was all over the place and included arrows referencing the neat rows. So, while the former said, "Mr. Antolini works on city council alongside fifteen other representatives," the latter interjected, "Typical pencil pusher." Practically every other sentence had a comment.

Henry finished reading the papers and Richard had him do some mic tests. Soon there was a knock on the door. In came Tom and a man.

Tom was pointing at the man. "Look who I found outside our door; it's our esteemed guest, Mr. Antolini." He turned toward Mr. Antolini and pointed at Henry. "This is the gentleman who will be interviewing you. Don't let his appearance fool you, he's a professional in every sense of the term."

Mr. Antolini put out his hand, and Henry nodded in response.

Tom said, "Have a seat, Mr. Antolini."

"All right." Mr. Antolini sat down while Tom went into the control room.

After about a minute of tinkering, Tom started the broadcast. "Ladies and gentlemen, coming up is our brand-new segment, the Golden voice, with your host, Henry. With him is our very own city councilor, Mr. Antolini."

The "on-air" light turned on as Tom pointed at them.

Mr. Antolini said, "Thank you so much for having me on."

Henry looked at his papers. "You work for city council alongside fifteen other representatives."

"That's right, we make all the important decisions concerning, for example, the water or roads –"

"I understand you also push pencils."

The on-air light turned off for just a moment. In the control room, Tom and Richard were wrestling for the controls; Tom had a wide smile on his face.

Mr. Antolini said, "I don't do anything of the sort. Right now, we're trying to zone for more offices."

"And how is that going to stop the war?"

You could hear Tom laughing through the glass.

Mr. Antolini's face was red. "It has nothing to do with the war. It's because the job market is changing."

"And why can't you find anything good to do with your time?"

The on-air light turned off for good as Mr. Antolini rose from his seat. "That's it. I won't stand for this." He stormed out into the lobby, where Henry could hear Richard meeting him. As Richard was pleading with Mr. Antolini in the lobby, Tom came in to Henry, wiping a tear from his eye.

"You know, those notes of mine, they

were jokes. You weren't meant to read them."

Henry gave such an earnest "oh" that Tom sprang back into laughter. When he had gathered himself, he said, "But I'm glad you did."

Richard threw the door open. "Nice going, you two. You just ruined us."

Tom said, "Relax, Dick, we aren't ruined. We just have to coach Henry a little."

"Coach him a little? He's absolutely lacking in human decency!"

Tom smiled at Henry. "You take the rest of the day off while we discuss things."

Henry left without a word and went to the library, where he sat until dark. When he came back, there was a crowd outside the studio. They wore the strangest colorful clothes, and they smelled. Henry walked past them to find Tom waiting for him inside.

"Hippies, Henry. The hippies love you."

"Sorry?"

"That voice always gets me; you should really talk more." Tom scratched his nose. "Do you know what hippies mean, Henry?"

Henry shook his head.

"They mean we can say whatever the hell we want. We don't have to coach you at all. As long as the hippies like you, you can be as rude as you want."

Henry smiled.

"Do you want to meet your fans?"

"Not really."

Tom chuckled awkwardly and led Henry upstairs. Then he made Henry stand right in front of the stained glass window, loosened a latch at the side, and pushed the whole thing so it rested horizontally above Henry's head. Henry had a clear view of the crowd below.

"Say something," Tom said.

"What?"

"Something about the man. Something bad."

"Who's the man?"

"Like the big man, society's man."

Henry had read something about him. He fetched a couple of his books and recited. "The first man who fenced in a piece of land and said, 'This is mine,' that man was the true founder of civil society. Beware of listening to this impostor; you are undone if you forget that the fruits of the earth belong to us all and the earth itself to nobody."

The crowd stirred a little, and one of them said, "Hey, it's the golden voice guy." But they looked bemused after his speech.

Henry leafed through another book. "Workers of the world unite; you have nothing to lose but your chains."

Someone shouted. "We don't work, though."

"Ok then. Tax the rich, feed the poor, 'til there are no rich no more."

A couple of people clapped, and someone whistled.

Tom tapped Henry on the shoulder. "Now, say something about them."

Henry cried out, "I'd love to change the world, but I don't know what to do. So, I'll leave it up to you."

The crowd chanted, "Golden voice, golden voice, golden voice."

Tom pushed the window back into place. "That was outta sight."

Henry went to sleep clutching his books. Maybe people would finally like him. And for his voice, at that.

* * *

The next month was busy. They interviewed a panoply of officials, everything from police officers to politicians. The more serious the person tried to be, the more irreverent was

Henry's response. Tom had plenty of notes on each guest, but there was no shortage to Henry's rebuttals either; they were more articulate. Between officials, they interviewed their fans; Henry let them do most of the talking.

Henry was reading on the sofa when Tom came upstairs with a band of Henry's fans and what Tom called groupies. Tom popped the cork of this huge bottle and pronounced: "Here's to one month." Soon the room was filled with smoke coming from some flowerless vase. The table was always full of bottles, and the couch full of women.

"You're so handsome," one of them said.

"And smart; look at all those books."

"Yes, he is. Say something smart for us."

Henry said, "Men make their history, but they do not make it as they please."

"Groovy."

Richard popped his head up from the stairs. "Henry, there's someone looking for you outside."

"Ok." Henry walked to the window, unlatched it, and threw it open. "Hello."

It was his parents. When they saw him, his mother sobbed, and his father yelled. "Do you realize how much worry you have caused your mother? If you don't come home right now, I will be furious."

"I don't care."

A few people inside cheered. Tom leaned out the window. "That's right; he doesn't care. And even if he did want to go back with you, he's signed a year-long contract with us." He winked at Henry and stumbled back inside.

"Is that right?" Mr. Vogler said.

"I'm not coming back," Henry said.

Mr. Vogler led his wife into the Bentley. You could hear her sobbing for two blocks.

* * *

Henry woke up to the front door being slammed. He found Tom in the lobby, rubbing his forehead. "Hey, Henry. Turns out I had promised old Dick a break. It's just gonna be us for a while."

Two weeks into Richard's break, things were looking a little different. The control room was always filled with smoke, and Tom kept wads of money on the table in there. He said it looked boss. Henry's fans hung out inside the studio now. There were always some in the recording room, even when Henry conducted his interviews.

Henry was about to say, "That is an asinine propagation of a capitalist patriarchy," for the seventh time that week when he stopped himself. This gave his interviewee a chance to explain why the city needed public transport. When the interviewee had finished, Henry just looked at him.

Tom said, "Are you alright, Henry?"

"I'm tired," he said.

"Let's take five." Tom took them off the air and beckoned Henry into the control room.

"Have I been overworking you?"

Henry said nothing.

"Alright, you're taking a vacation right now." Tom sent the interviewee home and Henry to his room.

Henry went to his room and stayed there for a week. Tom checked on him periodically, seeing if he was ready to work, but Henry had stopped talking entirely. He had forgotten how nice it was to be mute. It didn't feel worth the effort to talk. Tom's pleas changed nothing, and at the end of the week, in the middle of the night, Henry snuck into the control room, took all the money of the table in the control room and disappeared into the night.He had gotten the idea from a book. He took the late-night bus up north to a secluded town. There he bought a cabin from a certain Mr. Bartleby. Once Henry learned to work the land, he never had to talk to anyone ever again.

Mark and the Girl on the Ledge

ark was a plain-looking 34-year-old man. His mother never loved him, and he was still quite broken up about it. An untucked corner of his shirt fluttered in the wind as he stood on the ledge of a bridge from which he intended to jump and kill himself. Much like everything else in his life, he was procrastinating.

He wetted his index finger and held it in the air. "Southwest wind at about ten miles per hour. Upwards of sixty degrees. Chance of showers."

The bridge stood in a dense forest, where it had been abandoned years before. Mark half hoped it would crumble in a moment, sparing him the jump. A single drop of rain fell on the pro side of a crumpled-up list of pros and cons he held in his hand.

Cons: Need for decisiveness.

Pros: Easier in the long run.

He hadn't strictly found an actual con to put on the list, but he wanted to put something on that side. Besides, every argument in his head had been circling toward suicide for a while now, and logically, it seemed a lot easier to oblige. The problem lay in actually doing it.

Preoccupied as he was, Mark heard a timid pitter-patter of feet behind him and turned around to see a teenage girl.

"I didn't think there would be anyone else here," she said in a feeble voice.

Every article of clothing she wore was too big for her, so you couldn't see her hands, or that she was emaciated. But you could tell she wasn't energetic by how she could barely carry the brown satchel she wore over her shoulder. Mark thought she was pretty, which made him ashamed because she was kind of young. Not that he would do anything about it, he was just saying to himself that she was pretty. That didn't make him a bad person.

Mark realized he hadn't said anything in a while and blurted out, "Hi."

She straightened her back. "I came here to kill myself, but now that you're here, I feel sort of awkward about it."

"Oh… I don't mind if you want to go ahead."

She dropped her satchel. "That's kind of a strange thing to say to someone who just told you she's gonna kill herself."

"Well, what are you supposed to say?"

"Maybe something about how life is worth living."

"Oh." Mark hadn't thought about that.

She got up on the ledge next to him. "Do you think it'll do the trick?"

He held on to the arches and leaned down to see what was a drop that may or may not have killed them. Depending on where they dropped, the fall would have had upwards of a sixty percent chance of success.

"I think so," he said.

She turned to him. "What are you here for?"

Mark thought it over. He had no idea what he was doing anywhere at any time. As he looked at this girl, he wished that life was shorter. Not just because he wanted to be dead but because that way, he might remember what he was so upset about; it had all gotten so muddled up in time. Maybe the injury would still apply, and he could deal with it head-on instead of its lingering effects. This girl might have wounds so fresh that she could reach in and extract the shrapnel.

"I don't know," he said.

She did a poor impression of Doctor Phil. "That's no good. You don't have any direction in life."

Mark chuckled. "Is that so?"

"Sure is. You just have to ask yourself —" she thrust her index finger defiantly into the air — "what's the one thing you really want to do?"

Mark sighed, and for a rare change of pace, he actually told the truth. "I want to be a weatherman."

She looked almost disgusted when he said that. "Isn't that really easy?"

Mark burst into uncontrollable laughter. He had expected to defend himself for daring to be anything at all. "Honestly, I don't even know. What about you?"

"Ugh, why does everyone need to have a

thing? Can't you just be allowed to exist without having to be something?"

"You're the one who –" Mark felt himself getting frustrated, so he took a deep breath before answering, "I suppose you're right."

"What do you do if you're not a weatherman?"

"I temp at accounting firms. It sucks."

"Is that why you're suicidal?"

Mark wasn't surprised that she knew he was suicidal, even though he hadn't strictly told her. He imagined that everyone could tell everything about him just by looking. "I don't know."

"What's your favorite thing about being suicidal?"

"I'm sorry?"

"My guidance counselor told me that I could use a more optimistic view of the world. So, what's your favorite thing about being suicidal?"

"I don't know. I hadn't thought about it that way."

"Well, that's the thing, see I turned it over in my head and came to the conclusion that maybe it's a privilege in itself to feel tremendous pain. Not in a masochistic way or anything, but that maybe the pain is something that connects us all in a deeper way than even happiness could. At least that's the only thing I could think of that's positive."

"Then why do you want to kill yourself?"

"I just can't take it anymore."

The sky opened up and showered them with rain for a full minute before it stopped as abruptly as it had begun.

The girl jumped off the ledge onto the bridge and grabbed her satchel. "I'm going home."

"Just like that?"

"Yeah." She picked up her satchel. "Look, my satchel is all wet. Besides, you can't kill yourself on a rainy day."

Mark stood still on the ledge as she walked down the road. He remembered that he had predicted the showers and felt the slightest bit of pride. He stepped off the ledge and walked home.

He could always kill himself tomorrow.

Phaeton's Place

There were paintings lining every inch of the walls of this apartment on the twenty-eight floor. It wasn't quite the penthouse, but the apartment was easily large enough to room upwards of thirty paintings, Broden, its 22-year-old resident, and his roommate Dylan, who paid no rent. The two of them sat on a Nabuk blue, four seats, Baxter Leon sofa, at the far-right end of which was a pile of dirty laundry that Broden hadn't felt the need to pick up, as it had sat there the last four weekends, and no one had complained so far. He had even gotten laid one night.

"One out of four, that ain't bad," Broden exclaimed as he cracked open a Bud

Light later to stain the coffee table from the Arditi Collection.

"Yeah, but there were, like, four girls here every night, and we partied both nights. So, it's more like one out of 30," Dylan said without looking away from his game of *Call of Duty*.

"Whatever."

It was past eight o'clock, and they were expecting company at nine. So Broden cleared out the pizza boxes and, in an effort to "up his game," he lit a scented candle and placed it next to some empty beer cans.

The intercom buzzed, and Broden let in Trent and four girls in tight skirts and glittery jackets whose names all started with K.

"What's up bitches?!" Trent said as he burst through the door.

Broden grabbed their coats and nodded his head. When three out of four girls were already inside, he realized that in all the excitement, he hadn't actually said a word to any of them. So, he turned to the last girl while holding her coat and said, "Hi, I'm Broden."

She shook his hand. "Kate. The girls who just walked past you are Kylie, Kim, and Kendall."

"Radical."

She chuckled. "Do you live here?"

"I do."

She looked around. "I love the paintings."

"Thanks, they were having a sale."

"Funny," she said, in such a way that it was impossible to distinguish whether she actually thought Broden was funny, or if she was mocking him.

Broden hung her coat on one of the five empty coat hangers in the entrance hall. His own coat lay on his bed during the day and on his desk chair when he needed the bed. He turned his attention back to the girl, who was looking intently at one of the paintings.

"You like that one?" he said.

"I do."

It was a depiction of a young man in a leather jacket driving a convertible, to the back of which was attached a chain holding a giant ball of fire. Everyone in the flame's way was burning and screaming, and the driver of the car was getting zapped by lightning in the way that cartoon characters get zapped by lightning so that his head looked like it was being x-rayed. In the background, on top of a tall residential building like the one they were standing in, was a man that Broden liked to call "The Noodle Hair Man," playing a piano and singing "Goodness Gracious, Great Balls of Fire."

"What do you think it's about?" Broden said.

She pointed at the painting. "See the diner in the background?"

"Yeah."

"It's called Phaeton's Place."

"Right."

"Which means the painting is a contemporary rendition of the myth of Phaeton."

"Oh, cool."

She looked up at him as if that might mean anything to him, but he was preoccupied with the zapping effect, which he thought was cool.

"You wanna get a drink?" he said.

* * *

It wasn't until the Chatelet dining room table was covered in empty red cups, and the contentious but amateurish games of beer pong had settled into quiet chitchat that Broden made a sincere effort to learn the girls' names.

Kim was with Trent. Broden knew this because Trent said her name every other minute, which was technically a business tactic he had learned from his father, but it worked well on girls as well. It had something to do with establishing a connection with your subject. This was why it was important for Broden to know the name of the girl giving him the eye from across the sofa, but he felt it was too late to ask.

She was talking to the girl from the entrance hall, Kate. So, it wasn't Kim or Kate which left Kylie or Kourtney. The last one was with Dylan, but he couldn't even hear them talk. The girls on the couch were giggling now, which made Broden nervous. He sometimes got the sense that whenever people were giggling, they were secretly giggling at him – especially when it was girls. He had to do something, and that something was to scooch over and immediately lose all confidence in himself. "Uh, would you girls like a refill?"

The mystery girl looked at the floor in a practiced sort of way. "Are you trying to get me drunk?"

"Maybe." Broden had meant to sound coy, but he felt as if he actually sounded unsure of whether he wanted to get her drunk, which he did. Not like, in a creepy way, but in, like, a sexy way.

Kate shook her mostly empty Bud Light. "We'll have a couple more of these exquisite light beers, please."

"Coming right up." Broden went and got three Bud Lights from the fridge, and as he turned around to carry them back, the girl that had been talking to Dylan walked away.

Broden rushed over to Dylan. "What's the name of your girl?"

Dylan bowed. "And a good evening to you as well."

"Quickly, man."

"Alright, alright. It's Kylie."

Yes. That only left Kourtney. Or Kendall? No, it was Kourtney. He strutted awkwardly to the sofa and handed a beer to Kate. "Kate."

She nodded. "Thank you."

He handed another beer to the mystery girl. "Kourtney."

"It's Kendall, actually."

Fuck.

"I'm so sorry," he said.

"That's okay. Just come sit down next to me."

Broden crammed himself between her and the pile of dirty laundry. He caught a whiff of his stinky socks and felt a pang of shame. Why hadn't he cleaned up? There was nothing to be done about it now. He glanced over at Kate looking at the furniture almost as if she was window shopping.

Kendall ran her index finger down Broden's sternum. "This is a nice apartment."

Broden puffed his chest. "Thanks."

"What are you, like, a YouTube sensation or something?"

"No, it's my old man's place in the city. He's letting me use it while I go to school." Broden took little concentrated breaths to smell his stinky socks as little as possible.

"Oh." She took her finger off his chest and put it on her chin. "So, you're secretly a Brainiac, then?"

"Not really." Broden only went to school those days to keep up appearances.

"Shucks." She stroked the lining of the sofa behind Broden, then ran her hand up his neck and pulled his head toward her. "Well, I love the apartment."

"Thanks."

"You haven't shown me the bedroom."

Broden smiled. "How very rude of me."

They stood up, and Broden led her stiffly to his bedroom, which was easily as big as a studio apartment. Besides the coat on the bed, the bedroom was the only room in the apartment free of clutter. It was just small enough that Broden felt capable of keeping it clean. This is why he would sometimes hole up in there for days at a time, only leaving to get food and use the bathroom. The longer he stayed in there, the more he resented the rest of the apartment and his father for letting him use it.

"Look at those sheets." She jumped on the bed next to Broden's coat and frolicked on the Doppio Ajour sheets.

Broden wondered if he should just take his clothes off. She was in his bedroom. That was consent, right? He unbuttoned his top button.

She looked back at him and smiled as she lay stretched out on the bed. She looked really comfortable. Broden thought she looked like she was in an advertisement for mattresses or something, which was totally working for him. People in advertisements always seemed so happy and relaxed. As if they knew the secret to life and would whisper it in your ear for only 9.99$. Broden moved a little closer and unbuttoned another button.

Kendall pointed at the coat on the bed. "Take this away, would you?"

"Yeah, don't want this here." Broden grabbed the coat and threw it on his desk chair.

When he turned around, Kendall was sat upright on the bed. He jumped on the bed next to her and balanced his head on his left arm. "You're right, these are really soft."

She giggled. "Isn't this your bed?"

"Yeah, I'm just joking."

She leaned down next to him and observed the features of his face. Broden was about to inch up toward her and give her a kiss when she said, "Can I put lipstick on you?"

Is that like a sex thing? Broden thought. "Um, I guess."

"Yay!" She rummaged through her purse.

The various knickknacks in her purse

clinked against one another. Finally, she procured a dark red lipstick and started by applying it to her own lips, taking short glances at Broden in between looking at the small pocket mirror she held in her left hand.

After smacking her lips twice, she sat next to Broden and grabbed his face. He could feel her breath on his face as she brought the tube of lipstick to his lips and applied it with graceful precision.

"There, now you're beautiful," she said.

Broden moved his lips around to feel the wet layer of lipstick. He was trying to think of something sexy to say when Kendall stood up and rummaged through Broden's drawers. It was as well because Broden almost uttered the sentence, "My lips are so wet right now."

"What are you looking for," Broden said.

"We're going to play a little game," she said as she dug up a purple bandana.

"Alright."

"The game is Marco Polo." Kendall tied the purple bandana around Broden's eyes. "And every time you catch me I will take off an item of clothing."

"I like that game."

"Great." She tugged on the bandana to make sure it was tight.

Broden stood up carefully and extended his arms. "Marco."

"Polo."

It was to his right. He took one timid step and bumped his knee against his desk chair. "Fuck."

Kendall giggled somewhere in front of him. He pushed the chair away and lunged forward. Nothing.

"Almost had me there."

"Marco."

"Polo."

She was somewhere behind him now. He turned around and fumbled around in the darkness. As he did so, he heard a bleeping sound. It was the phone she carried in her purse. Broden lashed out at the sound and caught her arm.

"No fair. My phone gave me away."

"Still caught you," he said.

"Alright, I'm gonna take off an article of clothing. No peeking."

Broden waited and listened to the rustling of her clothes and the shuffling of her feet. When he could hear nothing anymore, he called, "Marco."

"Polo."

To the left. He stepped forward and fell flat on top of the bed. Somewhere in his periphery, he heard a faint clicking sound. "Marco," he said.

No answer.

He crawled to the end of the bed and sat on the edge. "Kendall?"

Still no answer. He lifted the bandana over his head. If she was still in the room, she would probably have chastised him. But there was no sound. And the bandana was so tight that he had to undo it from the back, which took him a minute. When he got it off, he saw without a shadow of a doubt he was alone in the room.

Maybe she had to pop out for a second. He stood up and looked at himself in the mirror. The dark red lipstick was uneven on his bottom lip. He was fully erect. There were still three buttons fastened on his shirt, and he undid them. Then he threw the shirt on his bed, walked around a little, drummed his fingers on his desk, and decided she wasn't coming back.

He got a rag from his closet and used it to wipe away most of the lipstick. Then he took the rag and smeared some of the color on the side of his lip and some on his neck. His erection had gone down by now, so he could go into the living room.

Dylan was alone by the table now, and Trent was still repeating Kim's name ad-nauseam. Broden strutted toward Dylan, and before either said anything, they high-fived. "Did your girl leave?"

"Yeah, everyone except for Kim left."

"Aight."

Broden felt it would be appropriate to smoke a cigarette shirtless on the balcony right now. Even though he fooled Dylan, he still felt like brooding over a cigarette.

"Hey Dylan, do you have any smokes?"

"Sure, they're in my coat pocket." Dylan took his phone out of his pocket and tapped away.

"Awesome, can I have one?"

"Knock yourself out."

Broden walked into the entrance hall, flexing his muscles ever so slightly when he walked past Trent and Kim. He rummaged through Dylan's inner pockets and found a pack of Marlboro Lights. Jackpot. On his left was a surprising absence of color. It was where the painting he and Kate were looking at earlier was supposed to be, but now there was a faint outline instead.

He stormed to Kim and jiggled the Marlboro Lights aggressively at her. "Your friends stole my painting."

"Whoa, what is going on," Trent stepped between them. "Are you wearing lipstick?"

"No." Broden rubbed his lips. "The noodle hair man is gone."

Kim leaned over Trent. "My girls didn't steal shit!"

Trent made himself even bigger by stretching his hands outwards. "Look, she says they didn't steal it. Are you sure you didn't just misplace it?"

"How would I misplace a painting?" Broden said.

Trent put his hands gently but firmly on Broden's shoulders and took him aside. "You're being very rude to our guest. If she says they didn't steal the painting, then they didn't steal the painting."

Broden got that feeling you get when you stand next to a tall building, and half expect it to fall on you.

"Now, if you can't treat our guests with respect, then maybe I'm gonna have to stop bringing girls over here. You like having girls around, don't you?'"

Broden swallowed. "Yes."

"Good." Trent let go of his grip and patted Broden on the shoulder. "And so, what if they did steal the painting? It's your old man's painting, right? I thought you hated your old man."

"I do."

"Well, then there you go." Trent took a cigarette out of the pack and put it in Broden's mouth. "Enjoy your cigarette."

Broden blew hot air out of his nostrils and walked past Dylan, who was pretending to have noticed something extraordinary on the floor in front of him, onto the balcony and shut the door.

Fucking Trent and his stupid fucking face. Broden lit the cigarette even though he didn't want it anymore. He felt stupid and naked and used. He coughed and wheezed, and he wanted to shout, but he didn't. Looking for something to kick, he found a beat-up portable grill on the floor and kicked the lid off it.

It was full of stamped-out cigarette butts. A whole mountain of them, some now littering the balcony. Come to think of it, that portable grill was the only thing in the apartment he had bought himself. He sat down opposite the grill and smoked his cigarette. When he was done, he flicked it onto the grill. Then he lit another. And another. Adding to the heap, he remarked sarcastically, "Goodness gracious great balls of fire."

Transfixed

Herman had a feeling. It was the same feeling that keeps people from meditating and relaxing on family vacations. Something between dread and restlessness. Thing is, Herman could have sworn he had never felt anything like it in his twenty-five years of life. In actuality, it had been building for the past month or so, but there was something about sitting in a musty basement playing video games at three in the afternoon that had permanently disrupted Herman's longstanding contentedness. So, he turned to his friend Alan and said, "I think I'm dying."

"Your health bar is full."

"I don't mean in the game."

Alan glanced at him. "You look fine."

"Well, I don't feel fine."

Alan paused the game and put down his controller. "Are you sick or something?"

Herman put his hand on his forehead. It wasn't hot. He didn't have a runny nose, he wasn't bleeding, nor was he in any physical pain whatsoever.

"I don't think so," he said.

The afternoon sun shone at an angle on the table in front of them. It would soon be prime video game time when the sun rose to the top of the basement and didn't disrupt the action on the television at all, but for now, it shone on bowls of half-finished cereal, a bag of chips, and a notebook with some meaningless scribbles in it, titled "Ideas." Alan stood up and walked to the mini fridge, where he grabbed a couple of yellow Gatorades and a bag of macadamia nuts.

He thrust the nuts and one of the Gatorades at Herman. "Eat this."

"Thanks, but I don't think —"

"You know, there's an art to slacking off." Alan made sure that Herman was listening, and seeing he was, he continued. "You still have to take care of yourself and maximize comfort while staving off ill effects. That goes double for mental stuff, by the way."

"Right." Herman opened the bag and shoved a handful of nuts into his mouth.

"You're still new to this, but you'll learn. Didn't you drop out like a month ago?"

"Yeah," he said between bites.

Herman had been in med school. During his first day of clinical rotations, he put on his scrubs, and instead of meeting his first patient, he left the hospital and drove home to his parents' house where he hid under a blanket for a couple of days.

"You're going to want to keep yourself topped up with healthy shit, like Gatorade, and nuts and such. Can't have pizza for every meal. That's why I have the Tower."

The Tower was comprised of five pizza boxes in the corner of the room. It was just under a red line on the wall over which it said, "One week's worth." It was now Thursday. Alan had Dominos deliver the pizzas through the basement window so his mother wouldn't see, but the recycling bin was always overfull with pizza boxes each week, so she still gave him a hard time. Herman suspected that was the real reason for the red line.

"Also, you need a routine. Do you have a routine?"

"Um, yeah."

Herman had a routine of sorts. It consisted of waking up before just noon and having a light breakfast of cereal and coffee. Then he spent the next hour goalsetting. This involved staring at a piece of paper for about an hour before he spent the rest of the day on idle escapism, which was anything from video games to jerking off to dick-girls. He didn't like jerking off to the dick-girls. He did it to upset himself without knowing exactly why. Then he wondered if he was gay, or if dick-girls were trans. Could a cartoon really be trans? If so, was he into trans? But he hated himself after jerking off to them. Did that make him transphobic?

"Great. You feeling better?" Alan said.

"I guess."

Herman felt a little better, but during the next two hours that they sat and played video games in silence, the Feeling enveloped him. The longer he distracted himself from it, the stronger it would come back. He doubted anyone else had ever felt this way. This wasn't true, but to Herman the Feeling was uniquely his, and that was the only thing that felt good about it. The Feeling. His Feeling.

Alan paused the game. "Dude you're totally throwing."

"I am?"

"I might as well be playing with a potato."

Alan chucked his controller on the couch. "Whatever, it doesn't matter."

"Is this because of that shit you were talking about earlier? You're worried about whether what you do matters? If you're living your best life?"

"Yeah, something like that."

"Hold on." Alan got out his Android. His home screen was a lewd rendition of Twilight Sparkle from *My Little Pony*. He typed something into Google and dialed a number. After listening to a short message he pushed a digit, and then another.

"How do you know if you're really alive?" Alan said to the person on the other side of the line. "Like, if you're really living life to its full potential or whatever."

"Dude, who are you calling?" Herman made an impotent reach for the phone.

Alan slapped Herman's hand away. "No, not a prank call. I really want to know."

Herman said, "What the fuck, are you actually bothering someone for this?"

Alan put his hand on the receiving end and said to Herman, "It's a government information type place, don't worry about it."

"Still."

Alan took a big hit on his Juul before hastily jumping back into the call. "Sorry, I'm being rude." He coughed a deep and grating cough. "Do you know someone that knows the answer?"

Herman stood with his hands in his pockets as Alan shook his head.

"That's alright. Thanks anyway." He hung up. "See, nobody has any answers; we're all just winging everything and you can play video games in peace."

Alan had picked up the controller when his other phone rang. His flip phone, which was easy to break in case of emergencies.

"Yeah, I'm holding," Alan said.

Herman wondered what sort of person could be calling his friend to buy drugs. Maybe he had a face tattoo or really baggy clothes and a mean look. Then again, Alan was the dealer, and he didn't look like a criminal at all. He was lanky with long hair and a patchy beard. He wore *Rick and Morty* t-shirts and spent an inordinate amount of time on Reddit. He used to brag about getting lots of downvotes, as if that was the point.

"I can meet you there. Let's say twenty minutes." Alan snapped the phone shut and turned to Herman. "We're going for a ride."

"Alright."

Alan opened a trunk strategically placed under the only vent in the basement to minimize the smell. He pulled a suitcase out from under a heap of blankets and bed sheets. It contained all the necessary paraphernalia: wrapping paper, a grinder, a pipe, and thick magazine paper cut into little pieces and bent in shape to be used as filters for joints. There were little bags, like the ones you get when you buy a couple of screws at the hardware store, with pre-measured amounts of weed sorted into one and two grams. Herman wondered if you could buy those bags in bulk somewhere or if Alan had to go and buy a ton of screws he didn't need. There were also a few rolled joints. He grabbed a two-gram bag and a joint and handed it to Herman.

"Take this to the car, the key is in the ignition."

"What? I can't do that."

"Sure, you can. I've gotta go get something." Alan disappeared up the stairs.

At least the Feeling was gone, replaced by nervousness about being caught with drugs. He had only tried weed once, and it didn't really take. Alan said that it was normal for it not to work the first time, but Herman always had doubts about trying it again.

Alan's parents would have been home by then. Herman put on his jacket and snuck upstairs. The front door was only a few steps to the left. He looked both ways when he came upstairs. All clear. The walls were painted white, causing the light to bounce off them. It was such a strong contrast from the dim basement it left Herman fumbling for his shoes when he reached the foyer.

"You heading out?"

Herman looked up from his laces. It was Alan's mom. He couldn't say where they were going. Actually, he didn't know where they were going.

"We're going to the shop," he said.

"Oh yeah? Where's Alan? I'm gonna ask him to pick up some milk." She looked down the hallway.

Hoping to end the conversation, Herman blurted out, "I'll tell him."

"Wonderful." She looked down at Herman and flared her nostrils a little.

"Right." Could she smell the weed? Herman stood up, and as he grabbed the door handle, Alan came walking down the hall.

"Alan," his mom said, "could you pick up some milk at the shop?"

Before Herman could interject, Alan said, "We aren't going to the shop."

They both looked at Herman, expecting an answer. "Might go to the shop. I meant to say we might go to the shop," he said.

"Should I go myself?" Alan's mom said.

"Probably best." Alan pushed Herman out the door.

Herman felt the cold autumn air on his face. Most leaves had fallen already, and the sun was cradling the top of the house on the other side of the street, a house which was the mirror image of the one they had just left. It cast a wide shadow across the street.

Alan opened the door to his 1992 Toyota Camry and stepped inside. "Why did you tell her we were going to the store?"

"I don't know, I panicked." Herman got

into the car and chucked the weed in Alan's lap.

As soon as Alan turned on the engine, the stereo played *The Dark Side of the Moon*. The cassette had been stuck for as long as he had the car; it was that or no music at all. Herman always jumped when the clocks chimed at the start of *Time*. He knew to expect them – he'd listened to the album many times over – but they still startled him.

They pulled into the parking lot of Bartleby Elementary. It was vacant except for a few empty cars. In the distance, a group of kids was playing basketball, hollering every time someone scored.

"Is this where you conduct your business?" Herman said, laying a sarcastic emphasis on the last word.

"Among other places."

A stubby red-haired kid walked down the road, and Herman was surprised to see him lean down at Alan's window. Alan cracked the window ever so slightly and told the kid to get in the car. The kid was hesitant, but eventually, he plonked himself in the back seat.

"What's the matter with you? Don't you

know you're supposed to get in the car when you're buying drugs?" Alan said.

The kid looked like he was trying to force his chin into his chest. "Sorry."

"What's your name?"

"Syd." He glanced at something outside the car to the left. In the distance, there were a couple of boys his age peering furtively around a corner. None could have been much older than fifteen, and none of them looked like what Herman had envisioned.

"Just be careful next time. Someone might see you." Alan chucked the bag of weed at the kid.

Syd examined the bag. "This isn't two grams."

"Yes, it is," Alan said without turning around.

"I know what two grams looks like, and this isn't it."

It was quite possible that the one- and two-gram bags had gotten mixed up in the suitcase, but Alan didn't admit that. Instead, he pulled an ancient-looking knife out of his jacket. It had two snakes entwined with one another on the hilt. "Are you calling me a liar?" he said.

The kid's face turned a sickly white. "No," he muttered.

Herman looked outside where the other boys had been, but they had disappeared. He watched as the kid handed Alan the money and how Alan counted it slowly before waving the knife at the kid, signaling he could leave. Once the kid had staggered out of the car, Herman turned to Alan. "Have you lost your mind?!"

Alan turned the key in the ignition and drove off. "Probably some of it, what with all the drugs and all. I wonder what happens to your mind when you lose it. Where does it go?"

He lowered the radio as he continued to muse. "Or is it more that you go mad and that I've gone, say, three-quarters mad? How do you quantify stuff like that?"

Seeing that Alan would not be serious, he changed the subject. "Where did you even get that knife?"

"It's a kila, I got it from my old man's office. And don't worry —" Alan ran his hand across the blade — "It's blunt."

"Do you know how many people go to the ER every day because of blunt objects?"

"No."

Herman shook his head. "Well, it's a lot."

"Don't you want to know what a kila is?" Alan seemed intent on changing the subject. Any subject that might imply responsibility on his half had that effect.

Herman sighed. "What's a kila?"

"It's like this ancient shamanic tool. Dad collects a lot of weird shit like that."

The entwined snakes on the hilt reminded Herman of the Caduceus. How the staff of Hermes had become associated with health care because some people couldn't tell the difference between the Caduceus and the staff of Asclepius. Unlike Asclepius, the god of medicine, Hermes was a psychopomp. It made Herman wonder whether those physicians who adopted the Caduceus were trying to heal, or whether they, like Hermes, were just carrying people to the afterlife. There were incurable illnesses. Plenty of ways to extort money from sufferers by extending their miserable lifespan. In such cases hospitals were at best a futility, or else an elaborate river Styx, complete with a cafeteria and validated parking.

They drove back to Alan's parents' house and parked the car a little away from it. Alan grabbed the kila and signaled for Herman to follow him with the same gesture he had used to wave away the kid earlier. It was dark now as they walked down a narrow road zigzagging past the naked trees. Herman stayed close to Alan, who seemed to know the way by heart. They came into a little clearing with a playground. A single light post stood in the middle and lit a sandbox, tire swing set, and seesaw.

"What are we doing at a playground?" Herman asked.

"A ritual," Alan said, "and we're doing it in a playground because there's never anyone here after dark."

Alan drew a circle in the sandbox and plunged the dagger in the middle. "You transfix the kila in the earth, thereby connecting our earthly plane with the spiritual," he said with uncharacteristic gravitas.

"And then –" he pulled the joint out of his inner pocket – "You blast off."

"Dude, are you gonna get high on a Thursday?"

"You know, in some places they call Thursday Little Friday." Alan sat down with his legs crossed. "And *we're* gonna get high."

Herman sat down and studied Alan as

he lit the joint, inhaled deeply and held his breath. Something about the meditative pose did suggest a ritual. Or a contentedness untouched by life's myriad worries. Finally, Alan exhaled and held the joint directly over the ritual dagger. Herman wondered whether there was just weed in the joint or if he'd mixed tobacco in there. He had heard that people did that, and he made a rigid point not to smoke cigarettes because of how unhealthy it was. But it wasn't as if it mattered at that point. Was it any healthier to smoke weed?

Also, if he didn't ask he wouldn't have to know. So, he took the joint and inhaled. As the hot smoke filled his lungs, he burst into a coughing fit. They passed it around again, and Herman anticipated what it would be like to be high. He lifted the joint to his mouth, but he didn't have it. Alan was polishing it off in the tire swing.

"How do I know if I'm high?" The words were foreign to Herman. He had said them, but the moment they left him they felt separate from him. As if someone else had plucked them out of his mouth and was now parading them in front of him.

"You'll know."

Herman lay on his back and attempted to melt into the sandbox. He caressed the cold sand, and as he felt it sliding through the space between his fingers more clearly than he'd ever felt anything before, he knew. He was, indeed, super stoned.

"You shouldn't have scared that kid. What if he's all messed up now?" Herman said.

"Is it my responsibility now to make sure people don't get messed up? People get messed up all the time."

"You don't have to try to mess them up, though."

"I'm not trying to mess anyone up."

It felt like an eternity passed between recognizing what Alan had said, formulating an answer, and actually saying it. So much so that any purpose had dissipated from the air, leaving only a vague feeling of discontentment. Eventually Herman said, "Right."

"Do you still feel weird?" Alan said.

"Yes."

"What do you think it is?"

Herman let the words fall out of his mouth without even thinking about it. "You know how you only get one life?"

"Yeah."

"Which implies that you only ever get to be yourself?"

"Yeah, I hate that. Like, I'll never know what it's like to have an old lesbian's tits, or what it's like to be a little French boy." He punched the air above him. "Life is so limited."

"Sure, but it's also, like, I only know how to be myself. And when I put on those scrubs, I felt like I was really going to be someone else. A doctor. Well, what would happen to me then? I know it doesn't make any sense, but it felt like I was going to die."

"Wow. That's deep."

"And now I feel that way all the time. Like I don't actually feel like I'm going to die, I just don't know how else I can describe it. But I don't wanna die."

"You're going to die either way, though."

"What?"

"You know, eventually."

Herman shrugged in the face of the truism. "Of course."

They lay and stared at the stairs. Marveled at their vastness and marveled at the sensation of cold. Marveled at anything, really. The dagger sat next to Herman, with the two snakes dancing out of the sand. He wondered how long people had been trans-fixed by snakes and death and misunder-stood psychopomps. For a moment he thought he had the answer to some impor-tant question, but when he tried to grab it, it slid through the space between his fingers.

"Huh," he said in amazement.

"What is it," Alan said.

"I thought I had something there."

Once the weed wore off a little, they went their separate ways. At home, Herman stood in front of his bathroom mirror and concentrated hard on being himself, what-ever that meant. When he found it impossi-ble, he vomited a glob of half-digested macadamia nuts on the toilet seat. As he went to clean himself up, he caught another glimpse of himself and laughed. He had been so afraid of losing hold of this creature in front of him. This creature with a runny nose and half-digested macadamia nuts run-ning down his chin. A little while later, after cleaning himself up, Herman sat down and felt the Feeling. It hurt. He cried. Then he went to bed, feeling silly and content.

Dolores

L ately, Dolores had acquired the habit of stumbling into various soirees and gatherings. Starting on Campus, she had gradually drifted away from the Village, then further up the Hudson River, toward the two-story upstate house of a lithe painter she had struck a conversation with at some art gallery or other a month ago because she felt their conversation was only half finished.

The house stood on a plot of land protruding into the river, along with two other delightful, if weather-beaten, houses. It was an outgrowth of land that seemed to have been misplaced beyond the train tracks. The roar of the river faded into the chatter of the house as Dolores followed a young man with gauged earlobes into the foyer.

"Merlin," he said and reached out his hand.

"Is it really?" Dolores shook it.

"No. But that's the fun thing about going to a party where you don't know anyone, you don't have to be yourself." He scanned Dolores. I'm gonna call you Teddy Coat."

"It's Dolores."

The man took off his coat. "Now, why would you tell me that?"

"I don't know, it's polite. And I actually know someone here."

"Touché."

Dolores turned her head abruptly to a painting in the foyer as if to say she was done with the conversation.

"I'll see you inside?" he asked.

She ruffled her pixie cut. "Mhm."

"Alright." He shrugged and disappeared into the living room.

The painting was one of those old-timey paintings where people seem to express a thousand things by the way their hand is positioned, and you can't tell what is being depicted unless you recognize that one dove in the upper left corner. Probably biblical. Dolores did not recognize this one. It was of an old man passed out in his tent and two beautiful naked women. Although ignorant of the origin story, Dolores knew the two women did not wear strap-on dildos in the original. She chuckled. Good on the painter. If old biblical paintings wanted to have naked women, then the least the painter could do was give them their own Signor Dildo.

Someone bumped into Dolores, who mumbled an apology for being in the way. She considered dropping the whole enterprise, but the little courage she had gathered at home in the form of a couple of tequila shots kept her from leaving.

Dolores left her coat on. As she stepped into the living room, an open staircase with a glass banister flanked her on the left. From the top, you could look over most of the living room. Next to the staircase was a table of refreshments. It had various cold cuts on one side and an array of drinks on the other. A little further to the right, hiding behind a fiddle leaf fig, was an upright piano, and at the other end of the living room, in a suburban houseplant jungle, various Sansevieria stretched upwards, and Monstera plants licked a semicircle of sofas upon which various bohemians from up and down the Hudson River lounged. It looked like one of them was wearing Mr. Mistoffelees from an off-off-Broadway production of *Cats* around his neck. There were suits at the party too, but they were all standing.

Dolores scanned the room for the hostess but couldn't find her. Feeling obliged to go somewhere she went to the table of refreshments. "I'm not really hungry," she said to herself and mixed a Skinny Bitch: vodka, soda water, and lime juice.

"Allow me to introduce myself. Chiron, the centaur."

Dolores turned around. It was the guy from the foyer. "Very funny."

He grabbed a cold cut with his fingers. "You aren't hungry?"

"I'm vegan, actually." She was not.

"Suit yourself." He munched on the cold cut. "Where's your friend?"

"Sorry?"

"You said you knew someone. Where are they?"

Dolores shrugged. "I don't know."

"Shame. Do you want to people-watch while you wait?"

"What's that?" Dolores said.

"It's where you look at people and give them a name and guess what they're like."

She stirred her drink. "I guess."

"Have you seen Mr. Furcoat?"

"Mr. Mistoffelees, you mean?"

"That's good," he said. "He goes to every production of *Cats* in the city with a rifle and hunts cast members during intermission."

She chuckled. "People like him are the reason for understudies."

"You're getting the hang of this." He pointed to an old woman wearing a fascinator made of half a bouquet of lavender roses. "What about her?"

"The Great Mother. Each rose is for a boy whose virginity she's taken." She looked at him coyly. "You better watch out if you don't wanna be part of that bouquet."

"Wow. Okay, I got one. Just walked in the door. The Professor."

A man with unkempt hair wearing a herringbone jacket with elbow patches walked in the door. He flitted about the foyer as if unsure of where to go. When he finally gathered himself and started toward the stairs, Dolores grabbed Chiron's hand

and pulled him behind the fiddle leaf fig for cover.

"I know that guy," Dolores said.

"Really? Is he actually a professor?"

"Yes, at Eversogreen. I go there." Dolores rolled her eyes at herself. "Actually, I used to go there."

Dolores watched the Professor walk upstairs and knock on the door directly behind the banister. After a little interval of the Professor fidgeting, the door opened, and he was greeted by a man wearing a stiff three-piece suit. Inside the room, Dolores could make out a desk and bookcase and was startled by a face that turned out to be a Venetian mask resting among the books. The two men went inside and closed the door.

"You done spying on the Professor?" Chiron had moved a tad closer.

She pushed him away. "Don't get any ideas."

"What ideas? I don't have any ideas. Besides, how am I to stop having ideas? They just come to me. Who even knows where they come from these ideas of ours?"

"Don't be obtuse."

"Sorry."

They stepped away from the fig. Dolores buried her face in her drink. Chiron rubbed his neck. "You know what, come here." He took her by the hand and sat her on the couch next to the Great Mother. Then he whispered in her ear, "Distract her."

"What?"

"Just do it." He sauntered to the back of the couch, where he pretended to play with the curtains. He bugged his eyes at Dolores and mouthed, "Do it."

Dolores bugged her eyes back and turned to the Great Mother. "I like your hat."

Chiron threw his hands in the air and mouthed, "Not the hat."

"It's a fascinator," the Great Mother carefully raised her chin to a ninety-degree angle.

"Yes, the roses," Dolores said. "What I really like are the roses."

Chiron snuck up behind the Great Mother, who answered, "They're from my garden."

"That's wonderful. Don't you love the variety of roses? Like, all roses are the same really but change the color, and you completely change the symbolic meaning."

"Indeed." She lowered her chin ever so slightly in acknowledgment of the comment.

Chiron was carefully pulling on one of the roses when the Great Mother lifted her right brow.

Dolores put her arm on the Great Mother's shoulder. "Like those lavender roses. Aren't you always amazed by a lavender rose? What even is that? I like them plenty, but they always seem a little off. Like, I almost expect them to be red because that's, like, the traditional color of a rose."

Chiron snagged a rose and signaled Dolores with a less than covert "ok" symbol.

"Actually," the Great Mother said, "these lavender roses are quite rare."

"That's so great," Dolores stood up. "But I have to go. Have a lovely evening."

The Great Mother let out an abrupt, "Likewise."

The couple retreated to the piano, trying to hold back their giggling. Chiron dangled the rose back and forth. "Boy, did we get her."

Dolores put her hands up. "Watch it with that thing."

"I want you to have it." He thrust the

rose at Dolores and cut her on the back of her hand with a thorn.

She stifled a frustrated scream. "You dunce."

"I'm sorry, is it bad?" He placed his hand on Dolores' wrist.

Dolores pulled her hand back. "You know what, I'm going to go find who I came to find."

"You want me to help you look?"

"No."

"Fine. Suit yourself."

Dolores grabbed a napkin from the table of refreshments and wrapped it around her hand while she tip-toed up the staircase. She could hear the two men arguing as she snuck past the home office and into a little den on the other side of the staircase. She sighed as she closed the door to the den, poured herself a glass of Bushmills 16-year single malt whiskey, and slumped into the purple armchair resting beneath a vivid, albeit incomprehensible, expressionist painting. From there, she tried to make out the titles in the bookcase. There was the *Social Contract* next to the *Leviathan*. Marx was leaning against Smith. And stacked in a neat line at the top was every kind of existentialist. It was as if the bookcase was having an ideological battle with itself.

No sign of her hostess. There had been something about her that made Dolores go all the way from her stuffy dorm room to upstate New York. Some way of looking at Dolores in precisely the way she wanted to be seen. At the same time, Dolores was putting off packing her stuff and moving back to her parent in Milwaukee since she had flunked every subject this semester. Even Interdisciplinary Studies: *a multicultural approach to critical theory seen through the lens of third-wave feminism*, which she found incredibly interesting, but couldn't understand at all.

Mr. Mistoffelees burst through the door and started rearranging the books. "No, no, no. It won't do."

He was wearing eyeliner, and his left hand (the one that wasn't rearranging books in someone else's bookcase) was busy playing at being a model in a commercial for male jewelry. He hummed incessantly, going through about three tunes in the minute Dolores spent watching the man before she coughed to get his attention.

"Hi there. Did you notice?" Mr. Mistoffelees sang.

"Notice what?"

"The whole house is in disarray. It's like they can't be bothered anymore." He saw the painting above Dolores and reached over her to adjust it.

Dolores stood up abruptly. "But you've made it crooked."

"Yes, well, it's the least I could do."

Dolores was overcome with a sudden need to rub her forehead, which is exactly what she did as she asked him, "Who are you?"

"An old friend."

"Whose friend?"

"Well, the couple's friend, of course."

Dolores just stared at him.

"Don't you know whose party you're at?" he said.

"Is it the guy in the office?"

"Yes, and his wife, the painter."

Dolores had an intuition about whom he was talking, and said, "Are they happy?"

"Happy?" He struck a pose as if he was soliloquizing in a play. "How could they be happy when the house is in disarray? He's in his office humoring some writer type, and she's probably in her studio. Meanwhile their guests don't even have any vegan hors d'oeuvres"

Dolores downed her drink. "Where is her studio?"

"Down the hall and to the right," he sang in a jarring falsetto.

Dolores left the den. The hallway was purple and dimly lit. There were more of those Bible paintings, and, as Mr. Mistoffelees had said, some were crooked while others were not. Just for the hell of it, Dolores skipped down the hallway, singing,

> "Every day's an endless
> stream of dildos and
> ketamine.
> And each time that I take a
> sniff,
> My dick gets hard, so very
> stiff.
> And every living thing I see
> reminds me that I long
> to be,
> In the ground."

She stopped at a door with a crooked wooden sign above it. The sort you made in woodworking class in school. It said "Studio." She opened the door and stepped inside. It was dark, and as she fumbled for a light switch, she tripped over a chord. When she finally got her bearings again and plugged the chord into the wall, a flood light blinded her. Once her eyes adjusted, she realized that every square inch of the walls was covered in paintings of vaginas. In the middle of the room was an empty easel, and in the corner was an orange futon.

"Wow." The abundance of the subject matter made Dolores feel like she'd been kicked in the ass with a heroin needle.

She kind of liked the paintings. Some were realistically pink, and others were various blends of unnatural colors. Some were lifelike, and others were comprised of layer upon layer of labia, stretching outwards and cradling the edges of the canvas. They were all signed *Ellen*.

"Do you like it?" It was her. The painter Dolores had come to find. She wore a V-neck dress and no bra. A single lock of her hair was curled, creating a chaotic loop down the left side of her face. She twirled it as she leaned on the doorframe.

"I do. It reminds me that it matters how you look at things. We might all be looking

at the same thing, but we see it differently."
Dolores said that to sound smart. She had
seen a similar exhibit of Les Femmes d'Alger
where she spent the whole afternoon trying
to find the best one.

"Very good. This particular exhibit is
called *drawing crazy patterns on your sheets*,"
Ellen said. "I heard you singing in the
hallway."

Dolores blushed. "I'm sorry, I was just
goofing around."

"No, I quite liked it."

Dolores balanced her head on the palm
of her hand ironically. "Well, I've been in-
spired by the greats."

Ellen chuckled. "They're all self-por-
traits, by the way."

"Excuse me?"

"The paintings."

Dolores burst out in awkward laughter
but stopped herself immediately. The feeling
was that of laughing in church. In fact, she
felt as if she was standing inside a shrine to
some capricious god that could either cover
you gently with layers of acceptance and understanding or swallow you whole.

Ellen kept talking as if she was con-
ducting a tour and nobody had done any-

thing inappropriate. "It's been a treat to paint something so personal. You saw my exhibit in the city?"

"Yes, I really liked the colors in that."

"Yes, of course. You told me," Ellen said, "Anyway, I don't think they'd ever put this on there."

"Fucking institutions."

"I know, right?" Ellen put her hand on Dolores' shoulder. "So, what do you do?"

In an awkward and spontaneous attempt to seem less bothered by what she was about to say, Dolores struck the same pose Mr. Mistofelees had taken earlier. "I'm currently flunking out of school."

"I'm sorry to hear that."

The readiness of the reply made Dolores slink down from her contrived pose and burst into tears.

"Hey, it's okay." Ellen led her to the futon and sat down next to her.

"I'm sorry. It's just that I don't know what I'm doing." Dolores choked on the sentiment. "And I don't seem to particularly want to be doing anything in this stupid world."

"That's alright, it's not so bad." Ellen eased off Dolores's jacket.

Dolores had several tattoos on her arms. Three birds taking flight, a motivational quote, and a few white lines running parallel to her wrists.

Ellen stroked her forearm. "I like your tattoos." She untied the napkin. "This one's recent."

"No, it's not like that." Dolores sobbed wilder than before, burrowing her face into Ellen's bosom. After a few sobs, she lifted her head. "You have really tiny titties."

Ellen looked down her dress and laughed. "You know what, I do have tiny titties."

They both laughed.

"My husband would like you," Ellen said.

Dolores straightened her back. "Oh. Is that the man in the office?"

"Yeah."

Dolores traced her finger along Ellen's thigh. Hoping to grab hold of some fleeting yet aching thought, she asked, "Why are some of the paintings in the house crooked?"

"That's a game we play. I hang them that way on the wall, and when we have company, Jonathan insists there isn't a crooked painting in the house."

"Why are some of the paintings not crooked?"

Ellen breathed a long sigh. "I guess someone must have adjusted them."

Satisfied enough with the reply, Dolores kissed Ellen on the mouth. Ellen put her hand on Dolores's cheek and leaned slowly out of the kiss. She slid her thumb across Dolores's lower lip. "What a beautiful mouth."

"Yeah?"

"I'd love to see my husband's cock in it."

Dolores backed away. "What?"

"Sorry, that sounded like it was straight out of a low-budget porno." Ellen stood up. "I just didn't know how to broach the subject."

"You can just drop it." She stood up and started toward the door.

Ellen grabbed Dolores's wrist. "Don't go, we'd be happy to pay you."

Dolores tried to yank herself free, but Ellen was surprisingly strong. "Stop it."

Ellen stood up. "Look, I'm sorry I said anything. I just figured… a girl like you might be up for something like that."

"A girl like me?"

"I'm sorry. Just… Relax."

"Let me go!"

"Okay." Ellen let go of Dolores, who fell backward against the wall. One of the vaginas fell down. It looked almost like it was staring up at Dolores. The floodlight was hot on her leg.

Ellen went to help her up, but Dolores instinctively balled her hand into a fist, punched Ellen in the face and ran out the door. Every painting in the hallway was crooked now. She bumped into Mr. Mistoffelees, who exclaimed, "Look, I fixed them."

"No, you didn't." She staggered through the den.

As she opened the door to the stairwell, the Professor stormed out the door of the office. "Thanks for nothing!"

Dolores stopped and waited until he had slammed the front door behind him before she shuffled past the open office door. Inside she perceived the Venetian mask but nobody else. She was at the head of the stairs when the husband stepped out of the office. They looked at one another for a moment. She thought of running out the door, but the

Professor would still be out there. Slowly and with great care, she walked down the stairs.

Some of the people had cleared out. The gauged earlobes guy was sitting at the piano, plonking softly on some of the higher notes. Dolores sat next to him.

"Mentor," he said, "pleasure to meet you."

"You're just a mentor now?"

"No, it's a character from the *Odyssey*."

Dolores hit a bass note out of beat. "I still think it's a little on the nose."

"Perhaps." He stopped playing and picked up a thornless rose that was dangling off the right-hand side of the piano. "For you."

She ran her fingers over the stem. "I liked it better with the thorns."

His face sank when she said that.

"But thank you," she continued.

He straightened himself, nodded his head in a rather bobbling way and plonked at the keys again. "You're welcome."

Ellen appeared in the stairwell upstairs and leaned against the banister next to her husband. He noticed a cut on her lip and stroked her cheek. She pushed him away and kept her eyes intent on Dolores. Someone turned on the light in the foyer.

Dolores leaned on Mentor's shoulder. "You know what you could do for me?"

He plonked with vigor. "What?"

"Walk me to the train station."

"Sure." He looked at Dolores's bare arms. His eyes lingered on her scars. "You have your coat?"

"No."

"You can borrow mine."

Dolores didn't protest, and they walked through the foyer and out onto the steps of the house, where the Professor sat smoking a cigarette. His right leg was tucked under the left as he leaned his head backward and blew smoke in the general direction of anyone who happened across him.

Dolores turned to Mentor. "You go ahead, I'll be right there."

"Sure." He walked to the side of the river and did jumping jacks in the chilling air.

Dolores sat down next to the Professor. "Can I have one?"

The Professor handed her a cigarette and lit it without looking at her much. She took a long drag of her cigarette before she started. "I'm sorry I got you fired, Newman."

He blew a lazy "What?" with the smoke.

"I was part of the boycott." Dolores stared at the train tracks in the distance. "You were here to get a book deal, right? Because you can't teach anymore?"

"You're observant."

She took another long drag. "No, I'm sorry."

The Professor smiled. "Were you a student of mine?"

"Yes. If it helps any, then I want you to know I'm flunking out."

"It doesn't."

"Oh."

"And you didn't get me fired. Not really."

Dolores rose to her feet. "Yes, I did. We boycotted your classes because you refused to problematize *The Ancient Mariner*."

The Professor stamped out his cigarette. "It's not like you stormed into the dean's office and demand that I be fired. You were basically part of a mob."

"Still."

"Still." He stood up and walked to his car. "Thank you."

His headlights cast a sobering light on the outgrowth of land upon which Dolores was standing. The river roared around them. She grabbed Mentor by the arm and let him escort her to the train station. It was the last time for a while that Dolores stumbled into a party.